THE DOXY AND THE DUKE

CAROLINE LEE

COPYRIGHT

Cover: EDHGraphics

ABOUT THIS BOOK

Lady Raina Prince might be the daughter of a powerful Highland earl, but polite society wants nothing to do with her, thanks to the illegitimate son she bore five years ago. She wouldn't trade wee Ewan for all the parties and musicales in the world, but when her old teacher, the Countess of Fangfoss, invites her and her five dearest friends to a summer house party, Raina can't resist the chance to see her chums again. She brings Ewan along as a reminder to herself, and everyone else, that she's not going to play their silly matchmaking games...and it works.

That is, at least until the day she takes her son swimming and meets a handsome and mysterious stranger enjoying the water with *his* son. What harm could there be in having some fun with a man who refuses to tell her his full name or rank? And if he thinks the worst of her...well, that could lead to some fun too!

The Duke of Cashingham has no time for frivolities, but he's given his heir, Matthew, his word that he'll make an effort to find a second wife. Thus, he has made a point of attending the Fangfoss affair to meet each eligible lady, and has been disappointed. But when he meets an intriguing—and obviously easy-virtued—Scottish lady by the river, he sees no harm in suggesting an informal liaison.

But the more time Cash spends with her, the more he realizes Raina is exactly the sort of woman he wants for a wife. Too bad a duke can't marry his doxy...

It's up to mischievous Ewan and studious Matthew to convince their parents that, not only are the two adults in love, but they have a chance at their very own Happily Ever After...before the end of the house party!

OTHER BOOKS BY CAROLINE LEE

Want the scoop on new books? Join Caroline's Cohort, an exclusive reader group! Or sign up for my mailing list by texting "Caroline" to 42828 to get started!

Steamy Scottish Historicals:
Those Kilted Bastards (3 books)
Bad in Plaid (6 books)
The Hots for Scots (8 books)
Highlander Ever After (3 books)
The Sinclair Jewels (4 books)
The Highland Angels (5 books)

Sensual Historical Westerns:
Black Aces (3 books)
Sunset Valley (3 books)
Everland Ever After (10 books)
The Sweet Cheyenne Quartet (6 books)

Sweet Contemporary Westerns
    Quinn Valley Ranch (5 books)
    River's End Ranch (14 books)
    The Cowboys of Cauldron Valley (7 books)
    The Calendar Girls' Ranch (6 books)

Click **here** to find a complete list of Caroline's books.

*Sign up for Caroline's Newsletter to receive exclusive content and freebies, as well as first dibs on her books! Or if newsletters aren't your thing, follow her on **Bookbub** for a quick, concise new release alert every time she publishes a book!*

CHAPTER 1

"It's a tiger? A lion?"

Raina Prince hummed thoughtfully and continued her invisible sketch on the naked back draped across her lap.

"Nay," she murmured, one finger drawing the curve of the feline's back. "But close."

Her wee son propped his chin in his hands and frowned as he concentrated on her touch, trying to feel the shape of the image. "There are whiskers, aye?"

"Aye, indeed." The gentle burble of the River Derwent, wide and calm here and excellent for swimming, seemed to echo throughout the perfect summer afternoon. "What else has whiskers?" she asked as she sketched the animal's fluffy tail.

"A dog has whiskers!"

Ewan was almost five years old, and visiting this part of the river had become a part of their daily routine. She would pack a picnic lunch, and they'd swim and eat until he was exhausted, then he'd nap in the shade of a magnificent oak while she read. But first she had to calm him to a restful state, so she'd invented this game where she drew pictures on his back and he tried to guess what they were.

"A dog does indeed have whiskers, my love." She drew claws beside where she thought she'd drawn the creature's feet a few minutes ago. "But ye were closer with yer guesses of lion and tiger."

"Oh! A panther!" Ewan guessed in excitement, thrusting his upper body up by straightening his elbows. "It's a panther!"

This wasn't calming him for a nap, was it?

Smiling gently, Raina wiped her palm across the lad's back, gently pushing him back down. "It's no' a panther."

"A jackal?"

Lightly, she pinched her son's bare arse, which wasn't as white as it had been at the start of the summer. Perhaps she *should* find him a bathing costume. But it's not as though anyone came to this remote bend in the river; in fact, it was almost at the end of the Fangfoss estate!

"A jackal isnae a feline, son."

"What's a feline?"

Hmm. Perhaps she ought to have a word with the nurse she'd hired to bring along on this trip. Annie was obviously not teaching the lad as much as Raina had hoped.

"A feline is a *cat*." To punctuate this lesson, she added a sketch of what she imagined might've been a dead mouse by the feline's front paws. "Like the barn cats back home."

When he still didn't pick up on the hints, Raina began

to stroke her palm across her son's back, as if she were stroking the cat's fur.

"Ye're certain it's no' a panther?"

She couldn't hide her grin. "Nay, it's no' a panther." The lad wasn't tired at all, was he? "But he's gray and white—"

"Like the barn cats back home?"

Ah, he was beginning to understand.

"Aye, just like the wee beasts," she murmured softly.

"Panthers are gray and white—"

"Nay, they're no'. It's *no'* a panther, Ewan. It's a feline who has just caught a mouse."

He pushed himself up on his arms once more. "Like the barn cats?"

"Aye," she huffed in exasperation. "Like the barn cats! He's gray and white like the barn cats, and he has whiskers like the barn cats."

"But how can ye be certain it's no' a panther?"

Raina's frustrated laughter burst out of her at the lad's dogged line of reasoning just as a new voice said quietly, "Is it a barn cat?"

Her son jumped up off her lap as Raina twisted to find the newcomer: a lad of about ten years in a bathing costume, standing quietly over her shoulder. He offered her a small grin and a shrug, as though he knew he'd startled her.

"Aye." She managed to find her voice. "It was a barn cat."

Ewan made an irritated sound and stamped his foot. "A *barn cat?* That was too simple, Mama!"

Hiding her grin, Raina busied herself picking up the remains of their lunch. "Ye didnae guess it. Our new friend had to."

"I *could've* guessed it if ye'd given me more hints!"

Wondering what further hints she could've possibly given him, Raina turned her attention to the newcomer. "And ye must be a smart lad to guess the drawing despite no' being able to feel it."

The lad shrugged again, his attention on Ewan. "Sometimes it's easier to see the whole picture from afar."

It was a surprisingly complex statement from one so young, and Raina was about to ask him about it when she heard yet *another* new voice.

"Matthew! Matthew, you win, lad! Where are you?"

The boy—Matthew?—flushed and whirled around, before calling out, "I'm here, Father. Already at our swimming spot!"

Our swimming spot?

Raina didn't have time to wonder about the claim before footsteps along the river path alerted her to the lad's father's arrival. And then she couldn't say a blessed thing, because her throat—and her lungs, and likely, her heart—seemed to freeze when the man stepped into the light.

He was *beautiful.* The man's pale hair glittered gold in the sunshine, and his tall, lean body was encased in a form-fitting bathing costume. She'd always had a soft spot for well-built men, and this one was no exception. From here, she could see the corded muscles in his forearms as he shifted the towels he carried to the other arm.

But his expression turned to confusion as his blue eyes swept over her and Ewan, and she watched as his eyes turned cool.

"Good afternoon," he said stiffly.

Instead of climbing to her feet, as though she and her son had done something wrong, Raina instead crossed her feet at the ankles and rested her weight on her palms. She saw the man's gaze travel down the length of her legs encased in dark wool, which was so popular for ladies to swim in these days, before lingering on her bare feet.

She wriggled her toes and was rewarded when he cleared his throat and glanced away.

"Have ye come to swim then?" she asked cheekily. "Do join us."

Although she'd been hoping Ewan would nap, he seemed even more energized by the newcomers' presence.

Her son rushed up to the new lad, Matthew. "My name's Ewan. I'm almost five, and I can swim! My granda says I swim like a fish, but I cannae breathe underwater."

Matthew nodded solemnly and offered his hand, as if unconcerned by Ewan's nakedness. "I'm Matthew, and I'm ten. My father says I'm a good swimmer, although the water here isn't over my head anymore."

Ewan shook the lad's hand enthusiastically. "Do ye come here often? Mama has brought me almost every morning this summer. Nurse says it's to keep me out of trouble, but I think it's because she loves me. Mama, not Nurse."

"You don't love your nurse?" Matthew was still allowing his hand to be shaken.

"She's alright, but she's no' Mama."

"I don't have a Mama," the older lad said solemnly. "She died when I was a baby."

So the golden-haired god glaring at them from the path was a widower? Interesting.

"I don't have a da," Ewan announced cheekily, "but Mama loves me enough for two, she says. Also, I have a million uncles and a granda and a barn cat. Do ye like it here? I like it here!"

Raina smiled as she watched Matthew—such a dear, serious boy—extricate himself from Ewan's enthusiastic handshake. "My father and I come here once a week in the afternoon to swim." He glanced over his shoulder at the gorgeous man who was slowly stalking toward the pair, and lowered his voice. "I don't get to spend much time with him otherwise."

Her heart clenched for the lad. Judging from the man's imperious gaze, he was some sort of local lord, likely too busy for much time with his son. But the fact he *had* made this time, and the fact they'd been racing here, meant he obviously loved the lad.

She was wondering if she should gather their things— and find some clothes for Ewan—and leave early in order to give the newcomers more time, when her son asked, "Is this yer favorite spot then?"

Matthew nodded. "It's the best for swimming. Father says *his* mother brought him here as a boy. And then he brought his little sister here—Aunt Carlotta—before I was born. But I've never had a friend to swim with before."

Raina's good-natured son smiled. "Now ye do! I'll show ye how long I can hold my breath, as long as ye dinnae let me drown. That's what Mama says." He whirled about with pleading eyes. "Is that fine, Mama?"

"I won't let him drown, ma'am," Matthew piped up.

Well, how could she deny two such adorable smiles? She couldn't drag Ewan away now, not by hook nor crook, with Matthew looking so excited for a playmate. "Have fun, the pair of ye."

The lads gave nearly identical whoops and lunged for the water. Matthew splashed right in, and Ewan flopped on his belly, coming up with a shriek of, "It's cold!"

"That's because you're naked, lad," the man murmured over her shoulder.

Knowing Ewan couldn't hear Matthew's father's chastisement, Raina assumed it was meant for her to hear only. But since she'd never been one to follow Society's dictates, she simply chuckled in response. Since she was still stretched out on the blanket, she tilted her head back and smiling at him invitingly.

"Will ye join me then, to watch our lads cavort?" As the man lowered himself to sit stiffly beside her on the blanket, her smile faded to a rueful one. "I'm sorry Ewan and I have stolen yer favorite spot. He's right in that I try to bring him here most mornings. We learned about the spot from one of the grooms at Fangfoss Manor."

When he exhaled, he seemed to lose some of the proper starch. Tossing the towels down beside him, he rested one elbow on the pile. "The Fangfoss property ends over there." He pointed to the next bend in the river. "I've been enjoying the shade of this tree since I was your lad's age."

So she was no longer on Fangfoss land? Whose land was this then? Did it belong to this intriguingly handsome man? Did she care?

Deciding the informality of the afternoon—her son was cavorting naked, by St. Columbine!—called for relaxed standards, Raina offered him her hand. "I'm Raina Prince."

He hesitated for a moment, then took her hand.

A tingly warmth—an *awareness*—encased her fingers and flowed up her arm toward her heart. She tamped down a shiver and met his gaze boldly.

Dear Lord in Heaven, but this man could make her do all sorts of things. She didn't know him, but she knew what she liked. And right now, she liked *him* very much!

"You can call me Cash," he finally said.

She cocked her head to one side, studying him, glad he hadn't released her hand. "Why? Is that yer name?"

He opened his mouth, but hesitated again. Slowly, as if considering his answer, he said, "It is *part* of my name."

"Then I have no choice but to assume your given name is Cassius."

From the river, his son's voice called out, "His given name's Adolphus!"

A laugh burst from her, and when the man pulled his hand away, she was immediately sorry. Instead of apologizing though, she offered him another smile.

"I think, were my given name Adolphus, I would choose to go by my family name as well." She guessed "Cassius" was his last name. "I apologize for giggling."

He shrugged and draped his forearms across his knees. "No one calls me Adolphus. I wasn't aware my son even *knew* my name."

She was surprised. "He's a smart lad, why would he no'?" Before he could answer, she teased him, "So I shouldnae call ye Dolly?"

She was relieved to see his lip's twitch upward as he snorted derisively. "I had an aunt who called me that. I hated it."

Glad he was accepting of her teasing, she said, "Then 'Cash' it is. It is better than Adolphus Cassius, which is truly horrible." She winked. "I'm pleased to meet ye, Cash."

There was something about the afternoon's informality which gave her the bravery to nudge his shoulder with hers. From the startled expression on his face, he hadn't expected it. He turned thoughtful blue eyes on her, considering his words, before nodding.

"I think I'm very pleased to meet you, Mrs. Prince."

Missus. The reminder he assumed her married should've been a bucket of cold river water over the warmth of the encounter. But she was far too used to the sneers of Society, and her body's reaction to him was *far* too intriguing, to be shunted aside by some flimsy reminder.

"Oh, ye should call me Raina," she corrected him. "Since we're being informal." She nodded to the river, where Matthew was trying to coax Ewan to sit on his shoulders. "Ewan, Matthew, Cash and Raina." She shot him a cheeky grin. "Just four people enjoying the summer."

He nodded slowly. "Yes. Yes, I think I should like that very much."

Out in the river, the lads seemed to be competing for who could hold their breath the longest now, but since Ewan couldn't count reliably past twenty, it was hampering the athletic competition.

"I *know* I was underwater longer than twenty-two seconds, Ewan!"

"I counted right!"

The older lad propped his hands on his hips, just visible under the surface of the river. "Show me," he demanded.

Ewan lifted his fingers and began to count. The higher the numbers, the harder it got. "Thirteen, fourteen, four-teen, sixteen, seventeen, eighteen, nineteen, twenty, twenty-one, twenty, twenty-eighteen, twenty-six, twenty-twenty, eleven!" he finished proudly.

Instead of being irritated, Matthew laughed and lunged for the younger lad, wrapping his arms around the lad's smaller chest, and catapulting them both into deeper water.

Suddenly alarmed, Raina sat forward, her eyes on the twisting swirl of water where they were playing, ready to spring to her son's rescue if necessary.

But a hand on her arm stopped her.

"Don't worry," Cash said in a low voice. "Matthew won't let anything happen to your son. He's a strong swimmer."

Nodding, Raina settled back on the blanket, though her attention never left the water. "And a good lad. He accepted Ewan as a friend immediately."

"He doesn't have many friends," the man admitted. "My position—"

He must've decided whatever he'd intended to say would mar the tranquility of the afternoon, so he bit down on his words. When she glanced at him—after ensuring both lads' heads were above water once more—he shrugged.

His grin was almost sheepish, and she decided she very much liked seeing him disarmed, instead of the cool and commanding personality he'd originally portrayed.

"I understand, milord," she intoned seriously, certain her eyes betrayed her mirth, as she made a point of lifting the edge of her bathing costume's skirt between two fingers and nodding solemnly. It was as close to a curtsy as she could get while reclined as she was. "Thank ye for lowering yerself to play with peasants such as ourselves."

The bark of laughter which escaped his lips seemed to surprise him, which caused Raina to grin.

"Ye *can* laugh, then?" she teased, which elicited more chuckles from him.

Finally, Cash settled back against the towels, more at ease now, as they watched their sons play. "I think, here, I'm not milord, and you're not a lady."

"Oh, I'm no' really a lady anywhere," she corrected him cheekily.

Her father was technically an earl—although Highlanders cared more about his title as Laird Oliphant—but her decisions five years ago meant no one in Society thought of her as a lady anymore.

Cash's eyes were twinkling speculative as they swept her relaxed and lounging form there under the oak.

"Really?" he murmured. "Lucky you."

Now it was her turn to laugh, just as Matthew succeeded in standing upright in the water with Ewan on his shoulders.

"Look, Mama! Look!"

Still chuckling, she sat forward again so she could clap appreciatively. "Well done, Ewan! Well done, Matthew! Can ye walk with him like that?"

It appeared not, as they were simply too unstable. But she liked that as soon as Ewan tumbled off Matthew's shoulders, the two of them popped right back up and tried again.

"He's a good lad," murmured Cash. "Your husband must be proud of him as well."

Ah. Well, the old gossip would need to be addressed at some point, but for some unknown reason, she didn't mind this man knowing the truth. Perhaps because of the odd instant connection the two of them obviously shared.

Or perhaps it was the desire she saw banked in his eyes, which she knew he could see in hers as well.

Shifting around to face him more fully, she held his gaze. "I'm no' married, Cash. Never was."

His eyes widened just slightly, before his gaze dropped to her lips. "Ah."

And now he thought her a whore, a doxy. A strumpet, a Jezebel, a harlot, a woman willing to part her legs for the right man, coin or no coin.

She'd heard the whispers for years. After Ewan's birth —after she'd refused to hide her condition and give up her son after his birth—Society had made it perfectly clear what they thought of her. It didn't matter that she was the daughter of an earl and sister to a viscount. It didn't matter that she'd attended one of the finest finishing schools in London. None of her skills or accomplishments had mattered at all, because she'd refused to hide such an important part of her life.

Her *son*.

Luckily, her family supported her in her decisions, and she'd been happy to retire to Newfincy Castle and thumb her nose at those who expected her to conform. But when the proprietress of her old finishing school—the newly minted Countess Fangfoss—had invited her and five of her closest school chums to Fangfoss Manor outside of

York, how could Raina have refused? She'd desperately missed her friends, and the chance to be together again outweighed the frustration of knowing the house party was an excuse to play matchmaker.

Well, it had worked. The former Miss Julia Twittingham was crowing over the fact that so many of Raina's friends had found love, and Raina knew she was being eyed speculatively. That was one of the reasons she'd insisted on bringing Ewan along to the house party; to remind Society, and herself, that she wouldn't conform to their standards. Not after they'd scorned her so thoroughly for following her heart when it came to her son.

As such, she made a point to take her son swimming, just the two of them. She spent time with her friends, but Raina refused to play the countess's games and attend the formal dancing each Friday evening. She would return home in the autumn still happily unmarried, but would rejoice in her friends' happiness.

And ignore the fact Society thought of her as being easy-virtued.

Well, perhaps I am.

She was surprised she didn't entirely mind that Cash— he of the remarkable forearms and chiseled jaw and warm touch—might think of her that way. There was something which very much looked like *interest* and *appreciation* in his eyes, when his gaze lingered on the neckline of her bathing costume, which lit a fire deep within her belly.

Nay, not her belly. *Lower.*

Trying to be as inconspicuous as possible, Raina

pressed her thighs together, secretly delighted at the spread of warmth which spiked through her. If she hadn't been sitting down, she might've gone weak-kneed.

Oh my.

Oh aye.

It had been a while since a man had made her feel this way, and even longer since she'd been tempted to *act* upon it.

Did it matter if he thought her a harlot? If he thought her available?

The way she was feeling right now, she wouldn't mind being *available* to this man. Not at all.

"Father! Look! We're doing it!"

"Mama! *Mama!*"

The lads' twin calls split the tension between Raina and Cash, and jerked their attention to the river, where Matthew was carefully feeling his way along the bottom, a proud Ewan clutching at his head.

Raina was, in some regards, relieved for the diversion. It wasn't as if she planned to attack the poor man just because she couldn't keep her arousal under control. But being reminded of her responsibilities had a sobering affect.

"Well done, lads," she called, knowing her voice sounded huskier than usual.

Cash was clapping and calling out, "Bravo! Bravo!"

Matthew looked surprised by his father's praise and grinned hugely, before attempting a bow, which of course sent Ewan tumbling forward with a shriek. Raina surged to her feet, peering anxiously at the water.

By the time her son's head popped up, and she felt she could breathe again, Cash was a warm presence at her side. And if she wasn't mistaken, his sigh of relief echoed her own.

In fact, the pair of them shared a quick grin as she lifted her arm to call Ewan out of the water. The camaraderie between them sent a surprising burst of longing through her.

What would it be like to share the worry and responsibility of loving a small human with another person? A *man*?

Did she want that?

Nay. *Nay.*

She'd tried to play by Society's rules and look where she'd landed. Better to remain thought of as a doxy, eyed in appreciation by men like Cash, than think about yoking herself to a man just so she could share some minor burdens.

And perhaps, while he was busy eying her like a delectable dish, she could do the same to him.

CHAPTER 2

NEVER MARRIED, hmm?

Adolphus Merritt, Duke of Cashingham, knew there were words for women who bore children out of wedlock, but he couldn't see how they applied to Raina Prince. He liked that she was so forthright, which certainly added to the evidence she wasn't exactly puritanical, but it was more than that.

She was kind and caring, that much was obvious, and she *teased* him. When was the last time someone—even Matthew—had teased him?

Never, that was when.

It's because she doesn't know you're a duke, you idiot.

Well, yes, there was that.

But when she'd been introducing herself and her son in such simple terms, Cash had resisted the urge to hide behind his title, the way he always had. Instead, he'd called himself *Cash*, which was a diminutive few were brave enough to use.

He was always, "Your Grace" or, "the duke," or more often, "the Duke of Cashingham, you know, the one with more money than Midas and a stick up his arse?"

Oh, he knew he was seen as imperious and cold, but that was a success, was it not? He'd worked hard to maintain that mien of aloofness his father had encouraged, and it had served him and his business dealings well.

Matthew was the only person he allowed himself to be...well, *himself* around.

But there was just something about this warm summer afternoon, with the sun shining merrily on the river, and this beautiful, refined woman, which made him want to be just *Cash*.

And she *was* refined. She might not be titled, but it was obvious she was well-schooled and understood social niceties, if only to laugh them off. She was far freer with her touch than any woman he'd met at a ball or musicale, or even the neighboring house party. And she made him *laugh*, which wasn't something to be easily dismissed.

She was fun to be with, and he wondered if he could convince her to spend more time with him. Perhaps horizontally—

"Are ye hungry, Cash?"

He blinked out of a fantasy where he was feeding her strawberries covered in crème, to see her offering him an apple. Grinning abashedly, he took it from her, noting her fingers lingered against his own.

And if he wasn't mistaken, the way her nostrils flared, and the subtle way she leaned toward him, all indicated she desired him as well.

Perhaps it was a good thing they were seated again, because this blasted swimming costume did nothing to hide his arousal.

Luckily, the lads didn't seem to notice anything unusual. They now sat cross-legged on the blanket, forming the last two points of their foursome, so that they faced one another. While their parents sent one another teasing grins and heavy-lidded glances when the lads' attention was elsewhere, Ewan and Matthew chatted happily about the river and the kinds of fish in it.

"Did you hear that, Mama? Matthew says there's fish as big as *me* in there! Can I see one?"

"Well, I dinnae ken," Raina answered smoothly, while handing her son an apple. "I've never fished in the Derwent, and I dinnae ken what we'd use as bait. After all, *ye'd* be far too big," she teased and leaned over to tickle him.

As the lad folded over in laughter, Matthew spoke up, in that serious way of his. "I could take him, ma'am. I'm a *good* fisher; my father taught me! And we'd use worms or cheese for bait, not little boys."

Ewan, still giggling, pointed at Raina. "Ye could help us dig them up!"

Although Cash suspected there wasn't anything which frightened this woman, she played along by wrinkling her nose adorably. "Touch slimy worms? *Me*? Nae, thank ye! But I'll hold the bucket for ye."

Matthew was beaming. "I could show you how to attach them to the hook. I'm *good* at that!"

He glanced at his father, as if seeking agreement. Or perhaps permission? Either way, Cash granted both, dipping his head in acknowledgement.

"Matthew once caught a fish *this big*." He held his hands about shoulder width apart, speaking to Ewan, and was gratified by the way the lad's eyes widened in wonder. "He wasn't much older than you are now."

"Was it here? Did ye catch it here?" The boy was bouncing in excitement.

Cash nodded solemnly. "Right here in this very spot. My son excels at everything he tries," he finished proudly.

As Matthew blushed and bit into his apple, Raina caught Cash's eye and grinned appreciatively. He was surprised by the surge of gratefulness which welled up at her approval. He didn't *need* anyone's approval—he was a *duke,* after all. So why did knowing he'd impressed her with his praise for his son make him feel all warm inside?

That's your cock talking.

Oh, right.

As Matthew launched into an explanation about the best ways to entice a trout, Raina's grin widened. Holding his gaze, she bit into the apple, and how in all the hells did she manage to make something so simple look so *sensual*?

The red of the apple matched her hair, which was speckled with gold in the dappled sunlight under the oak's branches. It really was a remarkable shade of red, almost fiery, and surely symbolized a personality to match. She wore it in a simple braid down her back, which had likely been for swimming, although small wisps of hair framed her face.

Although he knew she was likely a merchant's educated daughter, or perhaps a disgraced member of the minor gentry, he was struck by the simplicity of such a coiffure. She'd braided her hair to go swimming with her son, but what would she say if he offered her a maid to arrange her hair or drape her in silks?

What would she look like wearing nothing but those red curls and his naked body?

As if she could sense his thoughts, her hazel eyes shifted to a knowing look, and he found himself grinning in acknowledgement. Here and now, his title and her past meant nothing. They were two adults, enjoying the summer afternoon with their children.

"Tomorrow, Mama? Can Matthew teach me to fish tomorrow?"

He watched as her gaze dropped to her son's and saw the moment she understood what the question would mean. She opened her mouth to tell Ewan no, because Cash and Matthew only came to the river once a week.

But the thought of allowing that to happen—disappointing the boys, and in a very real way, disappointing himself—was abhorrent, so he beat her to the response. "Of course, lad. We could be here tomorrow."

It was Matthew who gasped. "Really, Father? Twice in one week?"

Cash shrugged easily, mentally reorganizing his schedule. "I think, if our new friends are willing to come tomorrow afternoon again, instead of in the morning, we could make that work."

While the lads celebrated in excitement, Raina dipped her chin in response to his unspoken question. She was so regal and beautiful, he damn near ached to learn more about her.

Cock, remember?

Damn, he must need some relief, because every movement the woman made caused him to stiffen.

"We can be here tomorrow afternoon," she said, in that soft Scottish brogue he was coming to love. "I'll pack enough lunch for us all."

Ewan was practically bouncing up and down. "I'm going fishing, Mama! I cannae wait to tell Granda and Uncle Phin!"

"Father," piped up Matthew, "do I have to wear a bathing costume tomorrow? Ewan swims in the nuddy."

As Cash choked on his laughter, Ewan smacked Matthew's arm. "*Ye* have to wear clothes because yer pecker's bigger than mine. Uncle Phin says I'm a wee lad with wee parts that willnae scare the ladies."

To Cash's surprise, Raina blushed, her freckled skin turning a becomingly pink tint. He hadn't thought anything could embarrass her, but apparently, her son's poor manners did. As Matthew defended the size of his "pecker," she groaned and dropped her face into her hands.

But once started, the rumble of laughter in Cash's chest didn't seem to want to stop. He was still chuckling as Raina tried her best to change the subject, and it almost worked.

In fact, his heart felt lighter than it had in...well, as long as he could recall. Usually, these stolen moments at the river with his son were the bright points of his week, but *today*...?

Today was special.

Even as he helped Raina pack up the blanket and the picnic basket, he had to fight back the uncharacteristic smile. He *should* be disappointed that their time was ending, but he'd been promised tomorrow.

And the promise of tomorrow was nestled in his heart.

SURPRISINGLY, Cash managed to accomplish rather a lot of things the rest of that afternoon, and the following morning as well. There was the usual pile of correspondence, and the household budget from his townhouse in London, where his mother and much younger sister Carlotta currently resided, but his secretary helped him manage much of it. Although the poor man *did* wonder at his employer's rush.

It was almost noon when he went to collect his son from the schoolroom, before stopping at one of the outbuildings to have the gamekeeper supply them with poles and buckets.

Thus loaded down, the pair of them began the hike to the river. It seemed closer today than usual, and Cash was cognizant enough to realize it was just his perception of things. This might also explain why he had been so eager to complete his business that morning.

He had a compelling reason.

One with bright red hair and an alluring smile.

Said smile—or rather, the memory of those lips around the apple—might *also* explain the vigorous hand-frigging he gave himself last night, but he supposed, as a gentleman, he shouldn't dwell on that.

It seemed his son was just as enamored of their visitors as Cash had been, although he assumed Matthew's interest was less base. The lad chatted constantly about his new friend on their walk, which made Cash wonder how starved the lad had been for companionship.

"Do you think Ewan and his mother are from the area, Father?"

"I doubt it, lad. We would've met them prior to yesterday were that the case."

"Do you think so?" Matthew hefted the poles higher on his shoulders. "I suppose, since they're Scottish, they could be visiting for the season. But it's possible they just don't travel in the same circles as you."

Cash twitched a brow at his son's observation. Had the lad turned into a bit of a class snob, then? He'd hoped, by keeping them both in the country—the far north country, at that—and away from Society in London, Matthew would grow to think of men as equal.

But perhaps not quite equal to you, hmm? Being a duke is second only to a prince really.

That was his father's voice, he knew.

"Well, lad, no matter her rank, I would expect someone as lovely as Miss Prince to stand out."

Matthew snorted softly. "That's true. I like her."

"I like her too, son."

The lad glanced at him when he said that, and Cash hoped his tone hadn't given away too much. But then they were at their swimming spot, and Raina and Ewan were already there. There was much exclaiming from the boys as their parents shared a smile, and they soon settled into the business of fishing.

While Cash supervised the boys in their attempts to find worms, Raina began to lay out the picnic lunch. She made them all wash their hands in the rushing Derwent, and even made a show of examining under Cash's finger-nails, which sent Matthew into peals of laughter.

Luncheon was surprisingly complex. No simple farmer's fare for Raina; she'd brought delicate tea sandwiches and fruit tarts and lemonade. If she had access to a kitchen to produce such delicacies, Cash began to wonder if she was a guest at one of the nearby manor homes. After all, she and Ewan obviously walked to this spot each day, so she couldn't be staying too far away.

Could she be...staying with a *man*?

Although she'd said she wasn't married, that didn't

mean she didn't have an arrangement with one of the local lords. Cash was honest enough with himself to admit he was already considering the proposition to her himself, and if she *was* taken, he was confident he could offer her enough to break off her existing liaison.

She didn't seem to begrudge him his deep thoughts as she teased the boys into laughter while they ate. She was *good* with them, and the thought sent a shot of longing through him he hadn't expected.

Before he had time to examine the reason behind it, he heard Ewan say matter-of-factly to Matthew, "Mama is the best Mama. And the funniest, and I have so much fun with her."

Matthew nodded as he bit into his tart. He was careful to wipe his mouth with one of the linen serviettes Raina had provided, before cutting his eyes toward his father. "I think having a mother like your mama must be the best thing in the world."

And here comes the guilt.

His son was subtle; Cash had to give him credit. But last year, he'd begun to hint to Cash he'd very much like a sibling, and when Cash—thinking the boy was old enough to have a frank discussion on the matter—had explained it wouldn't be a legitimate sibling without getting remarried, Matthew had asked him why he hadn't found another wife.

Somehow, the argument of, *"I don't have the time, and frankly, I like things the way they are,"* hadn't impressed the ten-year-old.

Cash might like things the way they were, with it being only him and Matthew together, but it was clear Matthew wanted more.

So Cash had agreed to put some effort into finding a new wife. Not *much* effort, granted, but *some*. He'd put it about that he wouldn't be averse to finding his name on a few of the local hostess's guest lists, and the matrons had been thrilled by the news. Of course, there was a limit to the number of social gatherings expected so far away from London, and he only accepted a minimum of invitations within those.

But in the spring, Matthew had asked again, and thus when the invitation to the Fangfoss house party had been delivered, Cash hadn't immediately dismissed it.

He'd been unwilling to commit to an entire summer of frivolity, and saw no need to do so. After all, his compatibility with a lady could be found after a single dance, could it not? That is how he'd found Amanda, his deceased wife and Matthew's mother, whose father had been a nearby landowner.

Thus, he'd written to Countess Fangfoss and announced his intention to attend her Friday evening affairs—dancing, most usually—in an effort to meet the lovely ladies in attendance.

From all accounts, the woman had all but fainted in excitement. After all, having a young, unmarried *duke* in attendance must have been quite the social coup.

But this week would mark the third such Friday he'd attended her affair, and each time, he'd danced with a perfectly lovely young lady…and each one had done abso-lutely nothing to interest him enough to ask for a second dance.

Not a single one of them had half the energy, half the blood-pounding *intrigue*, as the Scot sitting beside him on the blanket.

Of course, if one of those Society virgins had looked at him with the same heat Raina looked at him, perhaps things would've been different.

She continued to send him teasing looks as she collected the remnants of their luncheon—further evidence she was no pampered lady—and packed them away. Then she took one of Ewan's hands and one of Matthew's. "Well, lads, are we going to learn how to fish?"

"You, ma'am?" Matthew asked in surprise.

Cash watched as she squeezed his son's hand in excitement.

"Of course! I've heard ye're the best, after all, and as long as I dinnae have to touch a worm, I'm game."

The look she sent Cash made him wonder just how *game* she was.

Teaching her and Ewan to fish was surprisingly fun. He remembered when he'd tried to teach Carlotta, and the disaster *that* had turned out to be. He loved his younger sister, but she was much too talkative to appreciate a pastime which required one to sit quietly in the shadows and wait for fish to take the bait. As he recalled, that was the afternoon she'd attempted to climb the oak and had fallen out instead…

Raina, on the other hand, took to fishing quite easily, and eventually confessed in an aside to Cash she'd been fishing in Scotland since she was a girl. Ewan, on the other hand, lacked the patience and ability to stay quiet and in one place for long, which was required of a successful fisherman, but the lad certainly seemed to have fun chasing after the smaller fish in the shallows.

After a while, the two lads resorted to cavorting in the water. Since both of them were still fully dressed, Raina made them strip to their smalls, which had made Ewan—and Matthew—laugh in delight. She'd called out challenges, and Cash had to chuckle as he watched the two lads try to outdo each other.

"You are good at this," he murmured to her, as their sons tried to do push-ups under water.

She winked at him. "I'm just attempting to tire them out."

Sure enough, after about an hour, she called both boys up to the blanket and helped them dry off. Then she had them lie down on their stomachs, one on either side of her. Matthew pillowed his head in his arms and watched her.

Cash saw her smile gently at his son, then place her hand on his bare back. The lad shivered slightly, then closed his eyes as if in pain. Frowning, Cash wondered if he should interfere, but then Raina began to sing.

It wasn't that she had a beautiful voice, no, but her voice wasn't bad, and she closed her eyes while she sang the lullaby, low and soft and sweet. That, combined with the gentle breeze and the murmur of the river, made even Cash wish he might close his eyes for a moment.

Then she began to rub the boys' backs; not just Ewan, but Matthew as well. Cash saw his son's eyes flash open in confusion—being caressed so intimately by a near stranger must've been a surprise—but just as quickly, his eyelids began to droop again.

And why not? The combination of her lulling song and soothing touch must've been heaven. Knowing Matthew had been missing this softness in his life made Cash's heart clench; he now knew why the lad had asked for a new mother and regretted he hadn't found one for his son.

But it was impossible to think about getting married again to a *lady* when Raina was sitting right there. Raina who, were she a lady, would be an ideal candidate for the position: loving, accepting, and adventurous.

Doxies don't become duchesses.

The reminder didn't chill him as much as it should, because he was too caught up in the speculation of who she might be.

By the time she was halfway through her third song, Cash knew both lads were fast asleep.

Slowly, her voice faded to silence, and when he glanced up from watching their sons, it was to find her looking at him. There was so much he wanted to say to her, to ask her… She'd gone through all this trouble to make sure their sons slept, and he didn't want to waste it.

Instead of speaking, however, he pushed himself to his

feet and held out his hand in silent invitation. A flicker of surprise crossed her face before she reached up and took his hand.

The same warmth—energy, *electricity*—he'd felt yesterday washed through him at her touch, settling in his groin in a most inconvenient way. Or possibly the most wonderful way.

He'd never undertaken a flirtation with a child nearby, much less two children, but he would brave many things for the chance to touch Raina Prince. Silently, he tugged her out from under the oak tree, nearer to the river. Once he was satisfied they were sufficiently hidden from the lads, he settled his hands on her hips.

She was surprised again, he could tell, by the intimacy of his touch. But if he had his way, she'd be experiencing his touch much more frequently.

"Raina, I must ask you something."

Her fingers brushed against his shirt, exposed by his open waistcoat. None of them had dressed for swimming today, but they were still equally informal.

"Ye can ask," she murmured in agreement.

Be my mistress.

But now that he had the opportunity, his words floundered. How could he ask something so intimate, so potentially life changing, without being certain what her answer would be?

"May I kiss you?"

It wasn't until he saw the heat pool in her hazel green eyes that he'd realized he'd asked the question out loud, and winced at his awkwardness. He sounded like a schoolboy, infatuated with his first woman.

"I appreciate ye asking permission, Cash."

The gentle way she said it made him wonder if there'd been men who hadn't asked.

He swallowed. "And?"

"And I think I would prefer—if ye dinnae mind—if *I* kissed ye. I've been rather proud of my restraint thus far, to tell the truth."

He stopped breathing. That was the only explanation for why his lungs suddenly felt too tight, and it felt as if he were floating above his own body. He watched, somewhat in a daze, as she lifted her hands to cup his cheeks, before pulling him down toward her.

When she brushed her lips across his, her eyelids fluttered closed as if she were experiencing ecstasy, and he damn near moaned out loud.

But then she kissed him again, and his breath *whooshed* out of him, and he sucked in another breath so quickly, he almost went light-headed. But he quickly recovered and wrapped his arms around her waist, pulling her flush against him. When her breasts crushed against his chest, she made the most enticing little mewling sound of want, and the knowledge went right to his cock.

She kissed like a woman who knew what she wanted— a woman who knew what *he* wanted. No shrinking violet was she; Raina's lips and tongue kept pace with his until they were both gasping with need.

Cash couldn't ever recall a kiss such as this one; a kiss

which took him to a state of arousal so quickly he became dizzy. Or perhaps it was from the way all the blood in his body had dropped to his penis.

Yes, that's likely it.

Dear Lord in Heaven, but Raina could kiss! He knew he'd be hard-pressed to contain his desire for her, hard-pressed not to lay her right down on the riverbank and open her blouse and tease her nipples—would they be as pink as he imagined?—and taste her skin.

But he couldn't. Not with their sons—their innocent, trusting sons—so close by. Only the knowledge of Ewan and Matthew, sleeping peacefully on the blanket, helped Cash maintain some semblance of control.

It was difficult, but he managed to force himself to release her, to ease his hold on her. His only consolation was, when he pressed his forehead to hers in an effort to steady his heartbeat, her breathing was just as labored as his.

It seemed to him speaking would mar the moment, so he didn't. Instead, he focused on the way his palms pressed against her warm back, and the way her fingers caressed the side of his neck, and the way he could still taste her sweetness on his tongue.

"Tomorrow?" he finally murmured.

She straightened, then peered up at him. Slowly, her lips—swollen and well-loved—curled into a smile.

"Tomorrow," she agreed.

CHAPTER 3

SUDDENLY, this house party wasn't such a headache.

Up until now, Raina had spent a good portion of her days avoiding the society matrons the countess had invited to Fangfoss Manor, each determined to whisper malicious rumors about the *Scottish slut* and her bastard son. Raina had thus far managed to cry off attending the Friday evening dances Lady Fangfoss had arranged, so she didn't have to dance with the stiff and boring duke everyone was all atwitter about.

Each of her friends had been forced to dance with the cold and imperious man, and each had said it had been a horrible experience. There were times when it was handy to use one's ruined reputation to avoid social gatherings, and Raina had never appreciated that fact as much as she did now.

She still spent hours each day with her friends, but she didn't have to dread the countess's Mandatory Fun any longer, because she had something *else* to look forward to…and not just time with Ewan.

Weather permitting, Raina and her son still packed up their picnic supplies and walked to the river once a day, sometimes wearing bathing costumes, sometimes not. And sometimes they'd have an hour together before Cash and Matthew arrived, or sometimes the other pair didn't come at all.

She realized her heart was pounding with anticipation each day, full of hope she might see him, and she had to chuckle over her disappointment if he didn't arrive.

If he *didn't*, then the following day, he'd appear with flowers or a treat and a heartfelt apology for having to attend to business instead of pleasure.

The subtle reminder of his importance was just that —*subtle*—and Raina found it easy to ignore. She assumed he was some local lord, happy for a distraction from his usual schedule, and she was happy to be said distraction. Particularly because he was so delightfully distracting *her*.

She hadn't felt this attraction, this interest, in another man since…well, since the lesson she'd learned five years ago.

Oh, there'd been a few men here and there over the years whom she'd found attractive. But Ewan's father had taught her all sorts of things at a young enough age when she could still confuse lust with love.

There was no confusion now. She lusted after Cash, and no mistake. The man was temptation itself on two very finely built legs, with some other intriguing body parts tacked on as well.

She'd felt most of them in the times they kissed.

And they'd kissed plenty.

Although, the more time she spent with him, the more she realized she enjoyed spending time with him for *more* than just his body and his glorious lips—his *delicious, enticing lips*. She liked hearing his opinion on things, and she liked the way he thought through each conundrum carefully before expressing said opinions.

There were a few times when Ewan and Matthew were getting into trouble, and she deliberately didn't chastise them too quickly, just to see what Cash would do. And each time, she agreed with his decision.

She agreed with many things he did. He was obviously well-read and quite intelligent, although a stranger might not realize it, because he often had to be coaxed into discussions. One afternoon, the two of them and Matthew had a lively debate on the theme of Odysseus's travels, which resulted in much laughter, while Ewan stomped about, pretending to be a cyclops.

By unspoken agreement, they didn't discuss their lives outside of their spot under the oak tree by the river. He never asked how her days went after they parted, and she never asked what kind of business dealings had him frowning so heavily when he first arrived.

Instead, she would rest his head on her lap and rub his temples, smiling at the contented sounds he'd make as their sons swam and played together.

It was as though, there, it didn't matter who they were, or what others thought of them. There, she was just Raina, and he was just Cash, and they were parents to two wonderful lads who loved being in one another's company.

There, she didn't have to worry about her reputation or what others might think of her. In fact, because he didn't know who she was, she was free to be herself, and that included her flirtations with a handsome man.

Perhaps she should've learned her lesson with Ewan's father and hidden that part of her for the rest of her life. After all, her youthful indiscretion had led to years of being shunned by the very people she sneered at. But it had also brought her Ewan, and honestly, it wasn't as if she felt she was missing all that much to learn Society thought poorly of her.

Idiots, all of them.

Well, except her friends, of course.

Her friends, who were beginning to notice things were different with her after weeks of secretly meeting Cash and Matthew.

"You're looking cheerful," Angeline had teased her as they were preparing for one Wednesday afternoon's Mandatory Fun. "This is the first time you've actually participated."

"Aye, well..." Raina glanced toward the nearby window, where the rain was still pelting the panes. "I had nothing better to do."

Her friends, who knew of her daily trips to the river,

chuckled knowingly. Over the years, the six of them had shared so much—heartbreak, excitement, mourning, celebrating—and having them all together again was truly special.

But she hadn't told them about Cash.

Well, she'd mentioned there was a man who sometimes met her at the river with his son—she couldn't stop Ewan from speaking about Matthew, not with twelve yards of rope and a gag—but she hadn't said much about him. Perhaps it was Cash's secrecy, or perhaps it was the unspoken promise they seemed to have made to one another, but whatever it was, it seemed almost a betrayal to describe him or their time together.

But her friends knew, and often teased her about her good mood these days.

Of course, with it raining today—and yesterday, for that matter—it was almost impossible to be in a good mood. She hadn't seen Cash or Matthew in four days, and she *missed* them.

Last night, she'd tossed and turned in frustration, wondering what he was doing, as the rain beat down upon Fangfoss Manor's roof. First she was too hot, then too cold, and the blankets tangled about her legs. She wondered if he had the same trouble, and if he slept in the same ridiculous nightclothes she did.

In frustration, she sat up and tore her chemise off, relieved at the way the air caressed her body. Her hands had dropped to her breasts, imagining they were *his* hands on her skin, then lower. Her fingers had brought her relief, as they had many times before, but this time she had moaned *his* name.

"You're doing it again," hissed Olive as she hurried by with her arms full of costumes. "Staring at the window and smiling."

Oh.

Was she?

Raina's grin grew.

There was a *tsking* noise behind her, and she felt a hand on her shoulder pressing her into a chair. "Let me fix your hair," Charity offered, tossing a man's hat onto the table in front of Raina. "You never did care, did you?"

"No' even a little bit," Raina agreed cheerfully.

Well, that wasn't true; there'd been a time once, before her pregnancy, before her decision, where she'd *wanted* to fit in. But once Society had made it clear what they thought of her, she saw no reasons to meet their standards, and now took joy in thumbing her nose at them.

Which was one of the reasons she'd agreed to do this afternoon's performance.

"*Twelfth Night* is my favorite Shakespeare play," confided Charity as her nimble fingers braided Raina's hair close enough to her head that it could be hidden by a man's hat. "And I cannot wait to see you as Viola."

"Cesario," corrected Raina, running her fingers lightly along the century-old breeches they'd found for her to wear up on the hastily constructed stage. "Viola is Cesario in any of the scenes with Olivia."

Chuckling, Charity settled the tall hat upon Raina's

head and pinned it into place. "It's the confusion which makes the play so much fun. Besides, you might tell the others you are only doing this because it is raining, but *I* know it is because you adore the chance to shock the matrons." She pulled Raina to her feet with a smile. "And what could be more shocking than a lass in breeches?"

Raina made a show of stretching and examining her calves. "I do look stunning in them, do I no'?"

Her friend smacked her arse playfully. "You certainly do. Get out there and have fun!"

She and Angeline had prepared a series of scenes between Olivia and the cross-dressed Cesario. The first one, which was always one of Raina's favorites, now had the audience laughing as Raina tried to convince haughty Angeline of her master Orsino's love. Since Angeline—as Olivia—wasn't interested in Orsino at all, her mocking and teasing was appropriate, and Raina played poor Cesario as a hopeless fool just trying to do "his" job.

"Most sweet lady—" she began, but Angeline interrupted, as if granting him points in her little notebook.

"A comfortable doctrine, and much may be said of it." Her head snapped up, piercing Raina with a fierce glare above the veil she wore, as if she were one of the school mistresses they'd all dreaded years ago. "Where lies your text?" she snapped.

"In—in Orsino's bosom," Raina stammered, pretending to be cowed.

"In his bosom?" Her friend tapped her pencil impatiently against her paper. "In what *chapter* of his bosom, hmm?"

Pretending to rally, Raina acted as if she was parroting Orsino's words. "To answer by the method, in the first of his heart."

Angeline, as Olivia, waved dismissively. "I have read it. It is heresy."

While the audience laughed, Raina reached imploringly for her friend. "Good madam, let me see your face."

"Have you any commission from your lord to negotiate with my face? You are now out of your text!" Angeline snapped, but then seemed to relent. "But we will draw the curtain and show you the picture."

She made a big deal out of removing her veil, and as she slowly presented her now-visible face to the audience, there were even greater peals of laughter. Instead of using makeup to artfully enhance Angeline's natural beauty, Melanie had helped her cake on as many *unnatural* effects as possible; Angeline's nose was now twice as long, and sported two warts with great, disgusting hairs protruding, and even some of her teeth had been blackened.

Her fiancé Rothbury's shout of, "Oh, I say!" was drowned out by the rest of the company's laughter, which started up again at Raina's weak, "*Excellently* done, milady."

The scene, of course, required Cesario to compliment Olivia's beauty, while Olivia became more and more infatuated with "him." With Angeline prancing about, playing with her false nose and plucking at her chin hairs, it was almost impossible to keep a straight face.

More than once, Raina had to turn "upstage" to hide her own laughter.

They got through a series of other scenes, with Olivia declaring her love for Cesario, and Raina trying to fend off the poor woman. The last scene was always Raina's favorite, when Viola—still cross-dressed as Cesario—passionately explains why she can never love Olivia.

Angeline, as Olivia, of course, found it difficult to hear.

"Cesario!" She chased Raina around the stage, making hilarious groping motions. "By the roses of the spring, by maidhood, honor, truth and everything, I *love thee so!*" The laughter hid the rest of her line, but she ended up pinning Raina against a chair. "Reason thus with reason fetter: Love sought is good, but given unsought *better!*"

The script called for Raina to continue to reason with the love-struck Olivia, and they were planning on making it over-the-top comedic.

But for the first time, Olivia's words struck something deep within her.

Love sought is good, but given unsought better.

Raina had always understood that to mean that love could sneak up on you, which was, of course, Olivia's reason for telling Cesario. But suddenly, the image of Cash loomed in her mind, Cash's smile when he watched his son, or the intensity of his blue eyes as he argued his point during their luncheon discussions. Cash, with his remarkable body, and even more remarkable mind, who was never far from *hers* these days.

Love sought is good, but given unsought better.

She hadn't *wanted* to fall in love…but had she?

Damn and blast.

As the audience settled, Angeline's expression softened to one of concern. "Raina?" she whispered.

Raina shook her head, remembering where she was. Although this was supposed to be a comedic scene, she kept her voice low and intense. "By innocence I swear, and by my youth." She grasped Angeline's upper arms, causing her friend to gasp in surprise—which fit the scene —as Raina lifted her bodily out of the way, still holding her gaze seriously. "I have one heart, one bosom, and one truth, and that *no woman* has, nor never none shall be mistress of it, save I alone."

Perhaps it was her delivery. Perhaps it was the fact that so many people in the audience knew of her history, and her determination to, indeed, be her own mistress.

Whatever the reason, the silence was broken by a single set of hands, clapping intently, then the applause built and swept across the room, and Raina heard her brother, Phin—nominally at the house party as her chaperone, but really there so she could introduce him to her friend Olive—call out, "Brava! *Brava*, lass!"

In front of her, Angeline beamed happily. As if recognizing their scene was done, she threw her arms around Raina, who allowed herself to be hugged, and even returned the embrace. Then they both turned to take their bows and accept their accolades.

And through it all, a voice whispered in Raina's mind: *Love sought is good, but given unsought better.*

After the performance, she stopped by the nursery to check with Annie, Ewan's nurse, on the lad's studies and commiserate with the lad about the rain. She knew he missed Matthew as much as she missed Cash.

"That's alright, Mama. Me and Matthew can still play even if it's raining, 'cause we play inside too!"

She smiled and kissed him on his brow, loving his imagination. "Oh really, laddie? Where do ye play?"

"In our secret fort! I can't tell ye where it is."

Chuckling, she agreed that little boys should have their pretend forts, and wondered if the pair of them had built something near the bend in the river while she was preoccupied with Cash. She vowed to remember to look next time they were there.

To distract her son, she told him about the performance, even reenacting the funniest bits, and soon both he and Annie were laughing happily.

Feeling as if she'd helped distract her son from his boredom, Raina hurried to dress for dinner, deciding she didn't care for the stares she received for still being in costume. Once in her room, however, she planted her palms on her dressing table and stared at her reflection in the mirror.

She'd never pass as a man—which was what had made the scene so humorous, most likely—but in this light, she looked a bit like Phineas. She was pleased he'd attended the party with her, and now that he'd *finally* had the chance to make a connection with Olive, Raina hoped wedding bells were in the future for two of her favorite people.

In fact, wedding bells seemed to be ringing throughout the house party. First, Clementine had become engaged to Lord Dorset—it was a pretend engagement, which turned out to be real—and then that terrible Lady Farrah had snagged Mr. Howard, thinking he was a duke or something. Angeline and her Rothbury weren't too far behind, and now Olive and Phin were getting snuggly. And if Raina didn't miss her guess, Charity and Lord Wilton—two such opposites she'd never seen!—were next. And while Melanie never did what was expected of her, Raina suspected she had something up her sleeve as well.

Yes, all of her friends were enjoying themselves at this party, and more than a few had certainly found love.

"No' ye."

It wasn't until the image in the mirror blinked that Raina realized she'd said the words out loud. Scowling, she pulled the pins from her hair which allowed her to yank the hat off.

"No' ye," she repeated, holding her gaze in reflection. "Ye didnae come here to find love. Ye dinnae *want* to find love. Love is inconvenient and makes ye question yer choices." The woman in the mirror—currently dressed as a man, of course—nodded firmly. "Remember that," she cautioned.

Snorting softly at herself, Raina turned away and began to unbutton her waistcoat.

She was Ruined-with-a-capital-R, and she would do well to keep that in mind.

Though while there was a certain amount of freedom in being ruined, it wasn't all easy. Certainly, she had the freedom now to engage in a casual liaison with a handsome father by the river, and perhaps even do more than flirting. *But* she couldn't afford to think there'd be anything more between them. She couldn't afford to dream of love.

Lust had brought her to where she was today, and as a result, she could indulge in a bit of lust every now and then.

But someone like her wouldn't be allowed to love, even given unsought.

CHAPTER 4

ON HIS DESK at that moment, Cash knew there were three different reports from stewards at his various properties, seven petitions his secretary thought important enough for him to personally review, a letter to Prince Leopold of Bavaria which required his signature, and his mother's weekly missive, full of the London gossip and his younger sister's accomplishments, to which she would expect a personal reply.

Apparently Carlotta had managed to scare off her third music instructor—no surprise there—but had already gained the attentions of some earl's son thanks to her fine riding skills. Mother was enthusiastically planning Carlotta's presentation next season, which would either be a Smashing Success or a Giant Disaster, depending on how well his uninhibited sister managed to make her curtsey. Oh, and Mother made certain to include the fact her Precious Baby was growing up too fast and would become a woman soon.

Cash assumed this meant he'd be expected to visit London soon and either a) curtail Carlotta's wilder tendencies, b) escort the pair of them around Town, or c) give his approval—or disapproval—of The Match Of The Season. At least that was what Mother had called this hypothetical future marriage proposal in her letter, and he wasn't at all certain how he was expected to reply to that.

Yes, Cash had plenty to worry about in terms of his responsibilities.

So what was he doing standing in shallow water with his trouser legs rolled up to his knees, teaching a tow-headed lad one of the necessary skills for living in the country?

Having a far better time, that is for certain.

"No, Ewan. You have to curve your leading finger *around* the stone. Like this." He held the boy's hand in his. "Otherwise, you won't get the correct spin on it."

"I'm *doing* that!" the lad shrieked in frustration. "But it's no' *listening*!"

"The stone's not listening?" Matthew asked drily. "Have you tried explaining things louder? That might help."

Just as Cash sent his son an exasperated glance, Ewan lifted the smooth river rock to his lips, and screamed, "Ye have to skip! We're skipping ye! Skip, if ye ken what's good for ye!"

Matthew doubled over with chortles, and Cash hid his

smile as he nodded at the younger lad. "Yes, that should work. Remember to curl your finger around the edge, and try to hold it as straight as possible. You don't want to let it go on an angle—it has to be flat when it hits the water."

"Flat. Got that, Rocky?"

"You named the rock?" laughed Matthew, just as Ewan swung and released the flat stone. It skipped three times—a personal best for the lad—before sinking about ten feet out.

Cash immediately nodded and exclaimed, "Oh, well done, lad!" as Matthew clapped...but Ewan burst into tears.

"I miss Rocky! He was my bestest friend, and I *threw him away*!" he wailed.

Matthew's eyes were wide, torn between surprise and laughter, and Cash's brows went up. It was the lad's mother who came to his rescue.

With a no-nonsense manner, Raina joined them at the bank. "Ewan, focus. Ye asked Rocky to do his job, and he did it. He did it verra well."

"But I *miss* him!"

"Then go and get him." Her lips twitched. "Besides, ye ken good and well that Rocky wasnae yer best friend."

The lad's tears seemed to have magically dried. "Nay, Matthew is. Matthew, can ye fetch Rocky for me so I can try again?"

"I can..." Matthew hesitated, glancing down at his shirt and trousers. "I can fetch you *another* stone, if you'd like?"

Before Ewan could throw another fit—goodness, Cash

had forgotten what it was like to have a child young enough to require a nap—Raina tweaked her son's nose. "Strip down to yer smalls, lads, and I'll make sure yer clothing doesnae get dirty while ye swim."

Before Cash could even give his approval, both boys whooped and started divesting themselves of their clothes. Over their heads, Raina cocked a brow at Cash, as if asking his permission. He inclined his head in approval.

He was a *duke*. It wasn't just that he was used to getting his way, it was what was expected. His entire life had been full of people asking his opinion and suggestions and approval.

But here was a woman—a woman he knew nothing about—who had taken command of the situation, of his *heir*. Matthew listened to her and sought her approval in a way he'd never done with his nurses and tutors.

And Cash didn't mind at all.

"Will ye come swimming with us, Mama?"

"Oh yes, please, ma'am? And Father? Come swimming with us?"

Cash was in the process of rolling down his trouser legs when he glanced at Raina, fully expecting her to be the one to point out the fact they weren't wearing bathing costumes.

Instead though, she shrugged mischievously and offered them all a cheeky wink. "Perhaps. Go play while I hang up yer shirts."

It was strangely peaceful to stand there on the river-bank, his toes in the grass and the sun on his back. He was watching their sons play with half his attention, but the rest was on the gentle sway of Raina's hips as she arranged the lads' clothing over one of the branches, far away from the dirt.

He took a deep breath, held it for a moment, and then let it out. When had he last felt this way? Never, not that he could recall. There'd never been another woman who haunted his thoughts the way Raina did. When he wasn't with her, all he could think about was seeing her next, and when he *was* with her, he felt so at peace, it was almost scary.

His secretary was beginning to notice and comment on his more frequent absences. Cash had excuses for the man, but it was becoming obvious his daily attempts to sneak away to be with Raina, Ewan and Matthew were becoming problematic.

What he *wanted* was the chance to be with them all the time, which meant what he *needed* was for them to be under his roof at Cashingham.

He'd been thinking about that, in fact. If Raina and Ewan would consent to visit Cashingham as guests, perhaps once this idyllic summer began to wane, then he could have them on hand all the time.

He knew it wasn't done for a gentleman to keep his mistress in residence with him, not when his staff would know and judge. But on the other hand, what was the bloody point of being a duke without having the clout to flout rules a bit, eh?

If he wanted his doxy to live with him, to take her

meals with him so he didn't have to take time away from business in the middle of the day in order to make himself happy, who in damnation *cared*? Especially since he wasn't married anyway.

Easy, Cash. You're getting ahead of yourself.

He hadn't even asked Raina to become his mistress. Hell, he hadn't even bedded the woman yet.

But he had *plans*.

In fact, remembering that saucy wink she'd sent at the suggestion of swimming, he decided now would be an ideal time to put said plans into motion.

He sauntered toward her and happened to catch her just as she turned around. Her hands dropped to the waist of the simple dark skirt she wore. She gasped as she realized how close he was standing to her, but she didn't back away.

For his part, he resisted the urge to take her in his arms. "Well, Miss Prince? Are you willing to try your hand at swimming, fully clothed?"

They'd both gone into the river in the last weeks, but only when wearing one of those new-fangled swimming outfits, as they'd both been wearing the first time he'd met her.

Instead of balking, Raina's smirk turned naughty. Of *course* it did; she wouldn't be his Raina if she didn't rise to meet a challenge.

"Well, *Mr. Cash?*" she teased, putting just enough inflection on the name to remind him they hadn't been entirely truthful with one another. "Who says we have to be fully clothed?"

And just that quickly, her skirt dropped to her ankles.

He stepped back, shocked, and she chuckled. "Ye ought to see yer face."

"You really— You really intend to swim?"

She was still chuckling as she went to work on her blouse's buttons. "I'm wearing a chemise, am I no'? I'll be nae more scandalous than our lads are."

She nodded to where the two boys were cavorting; the water having stuck their light linen smalls to their pale round arses.

Cash swallowed, unable to stop imagining what she would look like with her wet chemise plastered to her curves and swells.

Bloody hell, he did *not* need a cockstand at that moment.

Looks like you're going to get one though.

She was already efficiently hanging her clothing from the same limb of the oak, and when she bent to roll down her stockings, Cash swore under his breath at the sight of her rear end framed by the soft material. He began to fumble with the buttons on his trousers.

If *she* was going into the river mostly naked, then by God, so was he!

She turned back to him and smiled in approval, which of course shot straight to his cock. He was enough of a gentleman to turn around as he undressed, but she still hummed softly as she gathered up his discarded clothes for him.

"Are ye coming swimming too, Cash?"

"Yes. I think the cold water will do wonders for me."

Her throaty chuckle told him she understood. "I think, perhaps, it might be safer if we swam in the deeper waters, so the water will cover us from prying eyes."

Since she'd slipped her hand into his and was leading him toward the river, he wasn't going to object.

"And are you a strong enough swimmer for such an endeavor?"

"Nay." She winked at him over her shoulder. "I'll have to hold on to ye."

Cold water cold water cold water.

Fortunately, there was something about an enthusiastic almost-five-year-old which could douse a man's arousal when necessary. Ewan insisted on climbing up on Cash's shoulders, while Raina taught Matthew how to squirt water from between his clasped hands.

Every once in a while, she'd look up and send Cash a secret smile, but the moment was sweet rather than sensual. He was struck by how easily she spoke to Matthew and how simple her respect was. She didn't treat the lad like a duke's heir—*because she doesn't know he is, you idiot*—but rather, as a boy who needed guidance.

And once or twice, when she reached over to move Matthew's hand into a better position or brush the wet hair off his forehead, Cash saw the lad close his eyes almost wistfully.

Was this what his son had been missing? A woman's touch, quite literally?

Cash frowned as he tossed a shrieking Ewan into deeper water and helped the boy bob to the surface again. He'd promised Matthew he'd take the task of finding another wife seriously, for just this reason. And Cash *had* been attending each of the Friday night entertainments the Fangfosses hosted, hadn't he? Was it his fault none of the Society misses presented to him held his interest?

None of them were beautiful enough, interesting enough, exhilarating enough, to convince him he could spend the rest of his life with them.

None of them were red-headed doxies, with a naughty streak a mile wide, who challenged him and made him feel like a good man.

None of them were Raina.

So yes, now that he thought of it, it *might* be his fault he was too infatuated with the woman currently coaching his son to look twice at another woman.

He needed to get her out of his system, get this fire out of his blood. He needed her, and not just a quick tumble, but a thorough lovemaking. *Then*, he was certain, he could get back to the business of finding a wife.

To that end, he needed to put his plans in motion. "Lads, come here. Have I showed you how Matthew can toss you, Ewan?" They gathered in water below Matthew's waist. "Place your knee like this, and Ewan, lad, you climb atop it. Hold his shoulders—Steady!"

Ewan squealed as Matthew was able to use that position to launch the younger boy into the air. Grinning, Cash made the mistake of glancing at Raina to gauge her reaction, and realized she was standing upright in water that barely reached her thighs.

The wet chemise was everything he could've hoped for.

The dark circles of her nipples—so they weren't pale pink?—shone through the linen, which clung to each curve of her breasts as if it were a second skin. As she clapped for the boys, Cash's gaze followed the wet, clinging material down her soft stomach to the shadows between her thighs, and suddenly, the temperature of the water mattered not a whit, because he had a cockstand which could've been used to shoe a horse, were an anvil not otherwise available.

Without stopping to breathe, he splashed through the water toward her and snagged her hand in his. They both half-walked, half-swam, to deeper water, before he turned her in his arms and settled his hands on her hips. The water reached below his shoulders, which meant she struggled to stand, but that was the point.

He dug his bare feet into the rocky bottom, braced his back against the gentle current, then lifted her so she could wrap her arms around his neck.

"There," he said with a satisfied nod.

"Why, Cash!" She pretended to be surprised. "Is it possible ye taught our sons a new skill in order to distract them so the two of us could cavort in deeper water in peace?"

They both turned to look at the boys happily practicing said new skill. "Cavorting?" Cash murmured. "Is that what we're doing?"

She pressed herself against him so his cock nestled against the junction of her thighs. "If ye want."

With a groan, he lifted her in his arms, her lips already straining for his. This kiss was just as magnificent as all the others they'd shared, but this time, Raina was plastered against him, her chemise hiding nothing from his bare skin.

One hand held her in place, while the other—completely unconsciously—cupped her breast through the linen, the water tugging at them both in the most erotic way. She made another one of those sensual sounds in the back of her throat and wrapped her legs around his waist.

Dear Lord in Heaven.

His cock was nestled right where he needed it to be, and thanks to this delicious folly, it felt as if nothing stood between them. He reached his hand down between their bodies and ran his fingers along her folds. She tightened her hold on his neck and deepened the kiss.

Despite the linen of her chemise between them, the sensation must've been what she'd needed, because Raina bucked against him and made a sound of *need*, which matched his.

How simple would it be to pull up her chemise and slip his fingers inside her? Or his cock? He knew she'd be wet and ready for him.

But their sons were right over there, likely giggling at

their parents kissing, and Cash knew a quick tupping upright in the river wouldn't be enough for him. He wanted the chance to take her, again and again, until he was sated. He wanted to see her writhe in ecstasy below him—hell, above him too—and hear the sounds she made as she came undone.

He shifted his grip so he held her by the thighs, a position which was pure torture for him, as he broke the kiss.

"Tomorrow," he gasped, echoing the plea from their first day together. "Raina, come with me to York tomorrow." Breathing heavily, he pressed his forehead against hers. "Can you get away and meet me there?"

She wasn't as quick to recover as he was, or maybe she was considering the ramifications. Either way, she eventually pressed a kiss to his temple and hummed in agreement. "Where?"

Thank God!

She was as ready for a tumble as he was!

"Nowhere important." He didn't want to be recognized. "There's an inn on the other side of the city, The Sword and Sheath, which makes some truly remarkable dishes." And the rooms were cleaned and well-appointed. "Meet me there for luncheon?"

And sport afterward.

Slowly she nodded and straightened away from him. "Luncheon, aye. I can get away for the afternoon as well." Good. She understood his intent, and judging from the eager look in her eyes, she approved. "But I have an engagement tomorrow evening, I'm sorry to say, and I'll have to leave in enough time to prepare."

Engagement?

What did that mean?

She had an invitation to attend something?

Or "engagement" as in a *man* had engaged her company?

Well, she'd been quick to say yes to Cash, and if Cash had his way, after tomorrow, he'd be able to woo her away from whatever protector she might already have.

"Is that acceptable, Cash?"

He startled. "Hmm? Oh, yes, of course. As it happens, I have an engagement tomorrow evening as well."

The blasted Friday dance at Fangfoss Manor, where yet another blushing debutante would be tossed at him for the obligatory dance.

In his arms, Raina shifted until she was holding his cheeks between her palms. The water swirled around them. "And tomorrow afternoon, after this remarkable luncheon, when the pair of us are safely hidden from small prying eyes...might we *then* discuss the length of oak wood currently pressed against my most sensitive area?"

Only his Raina could discuss something so intimate—so gauche—with such flippant ease.

Cash grinned. "I hope so. Oh God, I hope so."

Perhaps it was his fervent plea, or maybe she was just feeling silly, but Raina began to laugh; great peals of laughter, which drew their sons' attention. With Ewan clinging to his shoulders, Matthew began to battle the gentle current to reach their side.

As if understanding their interlude was over, Raina used her hold on his cheeks to pull Cash closer for one more quick kiss. Then, still laughing, she threw herself backward.

Since she was holding onto his face, and her legs were wrapped around his waist, Cash had no choice but to follow her into the water of the River Derwent.

They emerged to calls of, "Mama! Are ye alive?" and Matthew urging Ewan to be still.

As Raina half-swam, half-walked to take charge of her son so he didn't drown the older lad, Cash was filled with the most perfect sense of peace once more.

He tilted his head to the sky, closed his eyes, and joined in with the laughter.

CHAPTER 5

ONCE A WEEK, on Sunday mornings, Countess Fangfoss herded as many of her guests as she could into a group, and they all walked to the Cathedral in York. Raina had gone a few times on Phin's arm, but after a while, the whispers and pointed looks got to be a bit much, so she avoided that activity as much as she avoided the Friday evening dancing.

Unfortunately, the countess had told her explicitly, unequivocally, she was expected to attend tonight's entertainment. Raina had seriously considered faking a bout of the plague—it had worked to get out of that geography test when she'd been fourteen—or something equally dire, but had eventually dismissed it.

After all, Miss Julia had made it clear each and every one of her "ladies" was expected to entertain the blasted duke by dancing with him, and Raina had put it off as long as she possibly could. All she had to do was attend the one event, dance the one dance with him, and make her escape before the tongues began to wag.

The countess had it in her head that the duke, as the resident nobility, needed a wife, and she was just the woman to supply one. From what Raina had heard from her friends, the man was cold, aloof, cold, and far too haughty. Oh, and cold.

He sounds delightful.

But that was tonight, and Raina didn't want to dwell on the evening's entertainment, not when the afternoon's entertainment was bound to be far more interesting.

Interesting? Try invigorating, arousing, titillating, fulfilling—

She could likely continue, but her mind would eventually become taxed trying to come up with the more polite ways of saying, "I'll be making love to the most arousing man I've ever met," so she ought to just leave it at that.

Raina *could* walk to York, but she didn't particularly want to. Besides, she fully intended to be exhausted by this evening, and would appreciate not having to walk back to Fangfoss Manor. So she'd commandeered a barouche and driver for the afternoon, promising a generous tip if he returned for her at the appointed time.

And she was right on time now, as well. Her driver handed her down from the vehicle, and as she turned to enter the front door of The Sword and Sheath, there stood Cash. If she wasn't mistaken, his eyes were twinkling with excitement.

"You're early," he stated blandly, extending a hand as propriety demanded, his expression carefully blank.

Pretending to be a proper lady, she rested her hand atop his, feeling his warmth even through their *proper* gloves. "So are ye," she pointed out, deciding *being proper* could go hang. "I suppose each of us are...hungry."

His lips twitched as he escorted her inside. "Yes, indeed. I find myself *quite...* dot-dot-dot-*hungry*. I've been dot-dot-dot-*hungry* since I met you, Raina."

Raina. Not Miss Prince. Not ma'am. Not even *milady*. She was able to be herself around this man, and she loved that.

But not him. She couldn't love him, *because* of who she was.

Still, with a grin, she winked up at him, even knowing he likely couldn't see if under the veil she was wearing. "Then shall we find someplace private we could possibly dot-dot-dot-*eat?*"

He was already leading her toward the steps. "I agree entirely, my dear. I've had the liberty of ordering our luncheon delivered to my private room. I hope you don't mind?"

It was indeed a liberty, and if Raina were here for anything other than a thorough ravishing, she'd be shocked, positively shocked, to her core.

But instead, her grin turned impish. "I thought ye'd never ask. Lead the way, Cash."

So he did. She'd expected a private sitting room with a dining table, but instead, he led her to a bedchamber, likely the best in the inn. She stood in the doorway and lifted her veil to look around.

There was a dining table in front of the window, with a light repast already set up on it, but it was eclipsed by the large four-poster bed, with a number of fringed pillows, which took up most of the room.

Raina went breathless as soon as her eyes landed on it.

Behind her, she heard the door close, then the lock engage, but she didn't turn. She didn't turn when she felt, more than heard, him step up behind her, and she didn't turn when his breath tickled the sensitive skin under her ear.

"Raina," he whispered, "I've been waiting to have you for weeks. Are you certain?"

She closed her eyes on a quiet moan. "Cash, please—"

She couldn't manage anything else because her throat had suddenly gone dry.

Then he was in front of her, reaching for her hands. He took his time removing her gloves, pulling each fingertip gently to release them, and she shivered at the exquisite torture.

Intent on his task, he spoke without looking up. "I had planned to feed you first, Raina. Oysters and asparagus and chocolate, and all the other foods a menu might employ to help a man intent on seduction."

The first glove slipped from her hand, and he tossed it aside as he moved to the other.

"That sounds delicious," she managed.

"I'm sure it will be. But I've discovered I'm too impatient. Please, Raina…" The second glove joined the first, and he twined his fingers through hers and finally met her eyes. "Let me make love to you. Here. Now."

She grinned. "And save luncheon for later?"

"We'll need to recuperate our energy, I'm sure."

Pulling her hands from his, she reached for her buttons, pleased she'd worn a simple gown. "I find your proposition acceptable."

His grin flashed, and he shrugged out of his jacket.

Their clothing flew in various directions, along with barks of laughter as they realized how ridiculous they were being. But if anything, that only served to fuel their desire. After all, forget *oysters*…knowing he wanted her as much as she wanted him was a much more powerful aphrodisiac.

They fell into bed together, already tangled in one another's limbs, and Raina realized she was nearly frantic. Over the last weeks, she'd seen and felt his body—not necessarily naked, although yesterday's adventure in the river, wearing only their underclothing, had been close enough.

There would be time later to explore his body, to marvel at the smooth muscles and taut skin and that glorious vee which led downward from his abdomen, but for now, there only one thing she wanted to explore.

When her hand closed around his stiff shaft, Cash sucked in a breath, then exhaled on a groan.

"Lord in Heaven, Raina," he murmured as he dropped

his head back against the pillows. "You're going to kill me."

"No' yet," she whispered, lowering her head so she could brush a kiss against his chest, then lower across his navel.

His hand, holding her hair, curled into a fist.

"Not yet," he repeated, his voice hoarse. "I'm close enough already." As he spoke, his free hand reached between her legs. "And so are you."

It was crude. It was rushed. It wasn't the seduction Ewan's father had taught her to expect, but the hurried desperation of two people who'd been teased to the brink of bursting. Gasping, Raina shifted her hips forward, thrusting her wet core against his fingers, even as he used his hold on her to bring her breast closer to his mouth.

What was that about being close enough already?

She moaned as he teased first one finger, then a second, inside her, his tongue circling her nipple in an erotic mimicry. And then—*St. Columbine help me!*—Cash flicked his thumb across her clitoris, and Raina jerked in need.

"Please, Cash!" she panted. "Please!"

He didn't need any further urging apparently. They both knew this wasn't a seduction, but a culmination of something they'd both needed for so long. He rolled her onto her back, positioning himself between her legs, and took his long length in his hand. Her hands cupped her breasts, trying to recreate the sensations his tongue had caused.

With one hand braced beside her shoulder, he met her eyes. "Are you sure, Raina?"

In response, she reached up and draped her arms around his neck. "*Now*, Cash. Please!"

And then he slid home.

They both moaned at the perfection of the sensation, and she felt him exhale in harmony with her. They were still for a moment, and Raina basked in the feeling of being filled by such a remarkable man. It had been so long, and she couldn't recall the act ever feeling so perfect before.

And then he began to move.

Had she thought it incredible before? Each time he slid out—not quite free, but enough to make her miss him—he'd thrust back into her, and her inner muscles contracted around him in the most glorious way.

She planted her heels against the counterpane and allowed her knees to fall open. From this position, she was able to meet his thrusts, to undulate with him, and judging by his grunts, she knew he appreciated this new position as well.

In fact, it wasn't long before his breathing became harsher, and she knew he was close. She closed her eyes, willing him to find the pleasure he needed with her body, but he shifted above her, bracing himself on one arm again, even as he continued to thrust. Before she could open her eyes, she felt his hand between their joined bodies, felt his thumb against her clitoris once more. And when he teased it, her muscles contracted, and her orgasm burst over her in a surprising rush of delight.

She heard the moan emerge from her own lips, heard his echo, then felt him withdraw, leaving her empty and still pulsating. She didn't have time to mourn him, however, because he grasped himself in one fist, his knuckles brushing against her and providing the pressure she still craved, as he spilled his seed into the curls at the junction of her thighs.

Then he collapsed half-beside her, his legs still entwined with hers, the sticky results of their lovemaking binding their skin together. Raina's body was singing, humming, and she knew she needed *more*. More of this, more of *him*.

Luckily, they had all afternoon.

CASH COULDN'T EVER REMEMBER FEELING SO...*SATED*. He hadn't even eaten luncheon, by God, and he didn't care. He *did* rather care he'd gone after Raina with no more control or care than a randy lad, but she'd been willing to match him thrust-for-thrust.

Still, it hadn't been well-done, and he vowed, as soon as he had the energy, he'd make love to her slowly and perfectly, building up her anticipation until she cried out his name.

He grinned lazily against her skin, imagining that.

"I ken I should thank ye."

Her comment, coming out of the blue like that, surprised him enough to lift his head. "What?"

She was resting against the pillows, looking as boneless as he felt. Languidly, she gestured down her body. "For no'—ye ken. *In* me."

He blinked in surprise, glancing down at her curls—a deep red he hadn't taken *nearly* enough time to admire earlier—and seeing the evidence of his pleasure. It was a reminder.

As he rolled to the side of the bed and stood, he shrugged. "I know you already had one child out of wedlock and likely don't need another," he said as he reached the basin of warm water. He was wringing out a cloth and turning back to her when he saw a flicker of a grimace cross her face. "What?"

She sighed as he joined her on the bed once more, but didn't object when he began to clean her. He liked how unabashed she was with her body.

It was why he'd suggested this liaison, and why he had further plans.

"I would never trade Ewan, ye understand," she finally said quietly.

It was the *sadness* in her tone which jerked Cash's attention away from his lewd thoughts about future liaisons. He tossed the cloth toward the washstand and crawled up the bed until he could stretch out beside her.

"He's a fine lad, Raina."

Her soft smile had a hint of sorrow to it. "I ken it well. And ye have nae idea how happy I've been the last few weeks to see him playing with yer boy. Matthew is a brilliant lad and so good with Ewan. He genuinely cares for him, and Ewan craves that attention."

Before Cash could form a reply, Raina had rolled onto her side to face him, her expression intent. "And seeing ye with him?" She scoffed slightly. "Cash, ye are *such* a good father. Thank ye for sharing some of yerself with my Ewan."

To his surprise, Cash found his throat closing with emotion at the intensity of her appreciation. Until that moment, he hadn't realized how much it might mean to have someone else—someone besides Matthew—consider him a "good father." His own sire had spent little time with him, and while his mother had done her best, she'd been focused on attempting to force refinement on his sister in the years since Cash's first marriage.

But Raina... Raina had noticed, and approved, of how he parented Matthew. And it meant *so much* to him.

Cash had to clear his throat twice before he could form the words.

"You are welcome," he said hoarsely. "It's meant a lot to me to be able to spend time with him, and to see you with Matthew as well."

Solemnly, she nodded, then dropped her head back to the pillow. "I have three brothers, and they're all good men, in their own ways. My father too. Ewan is named after him. But none of them have quite made up for the lad no' having a father and brother. Phin thinks I let him run too wild."

"Who is Phin?"

She hummed. "Oh, my next-oldest brother. He's with me here at—in York."

Cash noticed her stumble, and wondered what she'd been about to reveal.

"And do you? Let Ewan run too wild?"

Her eyes were closed, her fingers idly tracing circles on her bare stomach, but she smiled softly. "Perhaps. Aye. But then, I allow myself too much freedom as well."

With a teasing growl, Cash rolled atop her, gathering her in his arms. "I *like* your freedoms!"

Chuckling, she wriggled beneath him until he managed to pull the counterpane over both of them and settled down with his arm around her. "What kinds of freedom do you think are too much, Raina?"

She was still smiling as her eyes closed once more. "I bore a child without the benefit of marriage, Cash," she reminded him. "My reputation—which was already battered because of my outspoken nature—was ruined after that. I suspect that, were it kenned I took my son and snuck out to cavort by the river with two friends, I would be chastised for that freedom as well. What else?" She hummed. "Oh, and in a recent production where I dressed as a lad, I paired a red waistcoat with a set of blue breeches."

Because he knew she was teasing, he chuckled, pulling her closer. "An outrageous freedom indeed."

But inside, his mind was whirling. Was she an actress then? She'd mentioned a production, and actresses enjoyed a certain amount of liberty when it came to their personal actions. He knew many gentlemen back in London who kept actresses as a mistress.

He'd had this suspicion, for a while now, that she was a member of the minor gentry, perhaps a gentleman's daughter—or even a lord's by-blow—who'd been led astray by a man who'd abandoned her after she'd become pregnant. But that didn't match the actress narrative, and the more he thought of it, the more he doubted that scenario as well; Raina wasn't a woman who would allow a man to hurt her like that.

When she stretched, her toes brushed against his, and he smiled instinctively.

"There are some who might say *this* is a freedom," she hummed appreciatively.

"It is indeed." He rolled so he could throw his free arm across her belly and found he liked the way her fingers rose to touch his forearm. "The freedom to do what we want, when we want. The freedom to be *who* we want," he added, thinking of the mound of ducal responsibilities he'd abandoned that afternoon.

Her fingers stroked from his elbow to his wrist, then back again, causing little frissons of delight to climb his arm and settle in his chest.

"And if ye could be anyone, Cash? Who would ye be?"

He answered without hesitation. "Your lover."

He *felt* her grin.

But something compelled him to elaborate. "I'd like to

be…just Cash. Just here, with you. None of the responsibility, just the chance to be like this."

She was silent a long moment, her strokes even and gentle, bringing him peace.

"We all have responsibilities. I dinnae need to ken yers to ken ye've allowed them to take over yer life. Even Matthew feels it."

It was true. Before this summer, he'd allowed himself only one afternoon a week with his son and heir.

As if understanding his thoughts, Raina continued, "Maybe all ye need is someone to remind ye to compartmentalize that part of yer life. Ye have responsibilities, but ye can also have fun. Ye can also be *just Cash.*"

The way he was when he was with her. When he was with her and Ewan and Matthew, all four of them together.

Sighing, he closed his eyes and rested his cheek against her shoulder. Her lips grazed the top of his head.

"I'd like to stay like this," he admitted quietly. "Being *just Cash.*"

Raina didn't know his full name or his rank or his responsibilities. She saw him as just a man.

"I'd like that as well. But remember, I have an engagement tonight."

Was *engagement* another word for a liaison? Or a theatrical performance?

And was Cash…jealous?

"I do as well," he sighed. "I've promised Matthew I'll find another wife."

She chuckled, which wasn't the reaction he'd been expecting, if he'd thought about it at all before stupidly blurting out the words.

"Nay, ye dinnae want another wife."

He lifted his head to frown at her. "I don't?"

"Nay," she repeated, moving her soft strokes to his knuckles now, and smiling gently at him. "Because then I cannae do this with ye again."

His brow twitched. If he married, he would have to end his liaison with her until he could convince her to become his doxy. "Good point. It *is* more fun to be informal."

She lifted her hand and pressed his head back against her shoulder, and he didn't resist. It was delightfully comfortable here, in this bed, in her arms. Instead of inflaming him, as he'd expected, her touch was soothing and exactly what he needed at that moment.

Of course, the bed wasn't nearly as comfortable as *his* bed at Cashingham. Could he convince her to join him there someday?

"Informality is essential sometimes."

Her statement confused him, and he shifted against her as he considered it. "In what way?" he murmured.

"Formality grants power," she explained, moving her gentle strokes up his arm once more. "A power over one another, but most usually, a power over the female."

Ah.

"Even with all the laws being discussed lately, allowing for a woman to own her own property?"

She pinched him lightly. "I should've kenned ye'd be involved in one of the Houses. Nay, dinnae tell me which one, we've kept our relationship *informal* up until now." In other words, she didn't want to know if he was a titled lord. "But aye, even with those laws in place. A woman is a reflection of her husband, and her husband's moods."

He was silent for a long while as he digested her words...and their meaning. Finally, he tightened his hold on her. "Is that what happened with Ewan's father?"

Her only response was a slight hum, and he decided to push her further.

"Will you tell me what happened?"

When she shrugged a bit too nonchalantly, he was almost dislodged. "What is there to tell? I thought I was in love with him, and he was verra handsome. But by the time I realized I was pregnant, I'd also realized what kind of man he was."

This was enough of a surprise that Cash lifted his head again to frown down at her. "What happened?"

Raina turned her head so she was staring at the window when she answered. "He did what he thought was the honorable thing and proposed marriage. I told him I had nae interest in yoking myself to a bully who used his power to hurt others. He gave me a black eye. I pointed out he was proving my point, and we parted."

Her tone was far too nonchalant, and the way she told of his abuse had Cash sucking in a breath. But he considered his words before he spoke.

"All this time...I assumed you had been abandoned by

Ewan's father."

A laugh burst out of her, and she sat up, dislodging him. The laugh hadn't been entirely joyful, but it wasn't hopeless either. At least she was meeting his eyes now as she patted his arm.

"Rather, let us say *I* abandoned *him*. I ken what I want out of my life, Cash, and I can imagine what it's like to be married to a man who doesnae love me. Did ye love yer wife?"

The question struck him as surely as a blade, and he reared back. "What?"

"It's a simple question. Did ye love Matthew's mother?"

He blinked and shifted in the bed, resting his forearms across his legs, more for a chance to think than because he was uncomfortable. No, he was already missing her touch.

"I...cared for her. She was a local girl, and I thought we would suit."

"Did ye?"

It had been almost ten years since Amanda's death, but he tried to remember their time together. Shrugging, he admitted, "Well enough, I suppose. We were married only a year. As I recall, she seemed much more interested in being a—" He bit down on the word *duchess*. "Well, she seemed more interested in making use of my assets than in me."

"And ye were interested in only her *assets* as a wife and mother, eh?" She nudged him. "She gave ye an heir."

He hated to admit it, but she was right. He and Amanda had had a marriage like many others in Society:

she had married him to become a duchess, and he had married her to beget the next Duke of Cashingham. There was nothing *wrong* with that, but he could suddenly see where it might, perhaps, be lacking.

He had a choice here. He could be affronted, or he could recognize Raina's point—and therefore her life choices—had merit.

Slowly, he nodded. "We suited, but no, I didn't love her. I like to think there were *merits* to being my wife, but I can see how you might not think so."

"Nay!"

Suddenly, she was kneeling in front of him, her palms on his cheeks, holding him steady so she could look into his eyes. God in Heaven, but she was magnificent with those beautiful red curls falling down around her pale breasts.

"Nay, Cash," she repeated, softer. "Whoever ye are, whatever role ye fulfill or title ye carry, remember this: as a man, ye are worth more. *Ye* are worth all the merit in the world." Her serious expression softened as her thumbs gently caressed his cheeks. "If a woman ever found herself lucky enough to be loved by ye, she should *insist* on marrying ye."

Slowly, she grinned and lowered her lips to his.

As he wrapped his arms around her and fell back against the pillows, half his mind was on the kiss, and the other on her words. *Marry?* When she'd just been speaking of informal liaisons? No, she'd only mentioned marriage in conjunction with *love*.

All he knew was, he needed this woman in his life. Doxy wasn't the right word for her; she was a strong-minded woman who knew what she wanted—*needed*—from life, and wasn't afraid to let Society's rules get in her way. But could he convince her to become his mistress? To do this more often?

"Cash," she murmured, her lips finding the skin of his neck. "I can tell when ye're distracted."

He was, wasn't he? Chuckling, he tugged at her until she was mounted atop him, her glorious red hair falling like a curtain around them as she grinned down at him. Her hands were planted on either side of his shoulders, and her plump breasts were close enough to cup. He loved how she was all curves, her body softened by motherhood and enjoyment of life. She was no young debutante—like whichever virgin the blasted Lady Fangfoss was going to toss his way that evening—but a flesh-and-blood woman who wasn't afraid to take her pleasure.

Just thinking of that *pleasure* had his cock stirring against the cleft of her arse.

His gaze on her breasts, Cash settled his hands on her thighs, his fingers inches from her curls. "I was just thinking of luncheon," he murmured, lying.

She hummed speculatively, shifting backward so their bodies were more closely aligned. "Ye're hungry, are ye?"

They had all afternoon.

He pulled her toward him. As their lips met, he growled, "For you? Always."

CHAPTER 6

"WELL, blow me down! Look at how well she cleans up!"

Raina's friends gave various exclamations of joy when she stepped into Charity's room for their habitual Friday evening pre-entertainment gathering, but Melanie's was the funniest. Brushing down the skirts of her least-favorite gown, Raina scowled at her friend.

"Melanie, dear, yer American is showing through."

Melanie didn't seem to care, instead staring in what could only be mock amazement, her hand on her cheek. "You're really coming to tonight's ball?"

Clementine spoke over her, waving her dismissively as she helped Angeline perfect her coiffure. "No one will be surprised by a little Americanism now and then, least of all her Frank."

"My Frank loves me exactly the way I am!" Melanie declared, whirling to scowl at Clementine, who waved cheekily. "We're *perfect* partners."

"In all ways," murmured Olive suggestively, her nose mere inches from her book. She did, however, peer over the top of it to sweep Raina with a gaze. "Please don't get her started."

Since Olive was soon going to be Raina's sister-in-law, she sent the shy woman a kind smile as she flopped down on the settee, not caring if she wrinkled her silk. "Believe me, friends, Melanie isnae the only one of ye lot who willnae cease prattling on about how in love she is!"

As this was met with laughter, Charity hummed loudly. "And you have not been waltzing about the manor, singing giddily?" She was peering at herself in a tall mirror, holding up first one necklace, then the other, as she tried to determine which one went the best with her lavender gown. "We have all been trying to determine which of the gentlemen has caught your eye."

"Who says it's a gentleman?" teased Raina.

Charity gasped and whirled around. "A *lady*? Raina Prince, surely you would have mentioned to us, your dearest friends, if you were canoodling with a *lady*?"

"Canoodling!" Melanie gasped happily. "*Now* who's sounding like an American?"

"Perhaps she did not know she was attracted to other women until we all practiced kissing one another that winter before we finished school, remember?" called out Clementine.

"Or perhaps she just prefers canoodling to rowing or sailing—"

Olive interrupted the sometimes-dim-but-always-good-natured Angeline. "Not *canoeing*, Angel. *Canoodling*."

As Raina rolled her eyes, Melanie waved them into silence. "I *think* she just means that the man who has caught her eye and made her so giddy—and don't think we don't notice you're walking strangely this evening as well, Raina!—isn't *gentle* at all."

Oh dear. It *had* been a rather enthusiastic afternoon, and Raina *was* feeling a bit sore.

"You mean he's a brute?" gasped Angeline.

Melanie clucked her tongue. "I *mean* he's not a lord. I swear, you British and your obsession with titles! When any man is worth as much as the next—"

"Yes, yes," interrupted Olive. "We all know Frank is a god among men, despite not holding a title." When she pierced Raina with a steady gaze, it seemed as if her spectacles magnified the effect. "Is that it then? Your lover isn't titled?"

Raina considered denying it, for all of a moment, before she relented and smiled. "I dinnae ken, honestly. I just ken him as a man, and he kens me as a woman, and we are quite well-suited."

"Well-suited?" hummed Charity as she went back to examining her jewelry choices in the mirror. "Is that what we are calling it these days? In that case, allow me to mention how *well-suited* Wilton and I are."

"And me and Rothbury!" exclaimed Angeline, patting her coiffure and turning to check herself in the mirror. "We go at it like rabbits!"

"What, with carrots and at a very young age?" Olive asked drily

Charity paused, one necklace suspended in midair, and burst into laughter. "I love how literal you are, Olive dear."

"Well, at least I didn't comment on Melanie's *blow me down*." Olive raised the book once more. From behind it came a mutter. "She sounds like a sailor."

Melanie winked. "I don't mind sailors at all, but I was just surprised to see Raina looking so gussied up. Normally she avoids these things."

"This is true," Charity called over her shoulder.

Raina sighed. "Go with the amethyst. It matches yer gown."

"Are you certain it does not clash?" Charity frowned at her reflection thoughtfully.

But Clementine was nodding, along with the others. "The amethyst necklace is beautiful and will not detract from your beauty, darling. Unlike whatever alarming concoction Raina is wearing."

Smiling happily, Raina fingered the elaborate embroidery on the skirt of her dark orange gown. "I ken," she agreed. "Is it no' hideous?"

"No," Angeline assured her. "It's a perfectly lovely gown and very much in style. Only…"

"Only the orange clashes with your hair," Melanie said frankly. "What were you thinking?"

"I was thinking I'd do just about anything to look ridiculous tonight."

Clementine made a soft, "Oh," of realization. "Tonight

is your dance with the duke, is it not? You could not avoid Miss Julia any longer?"

The chorus of corrections came from around the room. "*Lady Fangfoss, dear!*"

Raina's smile turned to a grimace as her fingers tightened on the silk, not caring she was crushing it. "The blasted woman cornered me yesterday and told me I was insulting the 'poor man' by avoiding my turn. As if he'd want anything to do with *me*," she snorted.

Sweet Angeline hurried to reassure her. "You are wonderful, Raina. Don't let anyone make you think otherwise."

"I dinnae think otherwise," she assured her friend. "I ken I'm wonderful, but I have nae interest in marrying a man just because he's a duke."

"What if you fell in love with him?" asked Olive quietly.

Raina's attention jerked back to her soon-to-be sister-in-law, and she sighed at Olive's naiveté. "I ken ye all believe love to be a magnificent force," she said quietly, moving her gaze around the room to encompass them all. "But ye also ken why I dinnae feel that way. If, in some strange twist of fate, I fall in love with a duke I've only danced with *once*, I still wouldnae allow anything to come of it."

They all knew her history and knew why she felt that way.

Clementine smiled sadly. "And if *he* falls in love with *you*?"

After only one dance? The idea was so ridiculous, Raina had to chuckle. However, she rested back against the settee with the smug smile her friends expected.

"Well then, my dears, that would be different, would it no'?"

Her friends chuckled at her knowing look, as she'd hoped, and dropped the topic, as she'd planned.

"Do be careful to lock the case, Charity."

Charity looked up from where she was placing the rejected pearl necklace away and nodded at Melanie's reminder.

Raina frowned. "Ye're no' afraid of thieves, surely?"

"No, but Ewan—" Began Angeline, before being hushed by the rest of the women.

Feeling her eyes narrow, Raina sat forward. "But Ewan *what?*"

She held Angeline's gaze, knowing the sweet woman would likely be the first to break.

She was right.

Angeline lowered her eyes, blushing. "He's a sweet lad. High-spirited."

"That he is," Raina agreed. "Has he been naughty?"

With a sigh, Olive snapped her book closed. "Since they won't tell you, *I* will. Ewan has been filching things."

Raina clenched her hand into a fist. "Expensive things?"

"Oh no," Charity hurried to assure her. "Just little knick-knacks. A portrait, a handkerchief."

"Dorset has not stopped complaining about the loss of his favorite hat," Clementine interrupted.

"I'd rather like to have my— Well, he's taken something small of mine," Melanie said.

"What?" Angeline asked innocently.

"Oh…just a small case." Melanie gestured the approximate dimensions. "About this big. It was enameled with a scene, so I could understand why a small boy might be interested in it."

"*Ooh*," Angeline hummed in understanding. "Your cigarette case."

Melanie blinked at their friend. "What? My— No, I don't smoke," she denied weakly.

But Clementine tsked. "Oh, don't bother with the protests, Melanie. We *all* know you smoke."

As Melanie tried to decide whether to deny it again, Raina was busy shaking her head.

"But Ewan wouldnae…" Raina trailed off, then closed her eyes on a sigh, remembering an afternoon in the library a few weeks back when her son had filched a pillow and book as he ran out. "He would, would he no'?" She rubbed at her temples, not caring what kind of mess she made of her coiffure. "But surely he's returned the things? After all, he's staying in the nursery. Surely I would've noticed an influx of men's hats or new pillows— and the book!" Wide-eyed once more, she glanced around at her friends, hoping for some explanation. "He cannae even read a full book himself!"

One by one, her friends shook their heads or avoided her gaze. Only Olive met her eyes.

"I'm sorry, Raina. We don't know what he's *doing* with the things, but we've all seen him run up and snatch something. He even took a pair of my spectacles."

"Aye, I believe it," Raina agreed with another weary sigh. "I've seen him filch a book and a pillow. But I assumed he was hiding in the nursery with his stolen goods and Annie would return them to their rightful place."

"I don't think that's happening," Melanie said carefully. "In fact, my maid told me yesterday that the cook's even been complaining because *food* has started going missing."

"Food? Why would he take food?" Olive scoffed.

Clementine winced. "I do not know, but Dorset's hat—"

"Oh, shush about the hat! Can't you see how upset Raina is?" hissed Angeline.

Offering a weak smile, Raina shook her head. "Nay, ye have a right to be irritated. I cannae believe I havenae noticed…" She dropped her head into her hands, rubbing at her temples once more. "I'm a terrible mother," she mumbled.

Suddenly, Charity was beside her on the settee, her hand on Raina's back. "You are a *wonderful* mother. We would all be lucky to be mothers like you or *have* mothers like you. You have raised your son to believe in freedom, and I have never met a more cheerful little boy."

Around the room, her fervent claim was met with

murmurs of agreement.

Raina huffed slightly, more touched than she wanted to admit by her friends' support. "Thank ye," she whispered, then straightened, smiling weakly. "I love ye all."

"And we love you," Olive replied softly, squeezing next to Raina on the opposite end of the settee. "And we love Ewan. But it sounds as if he's up to something rather mischievous."

"I heard it was plum pudding that went missing," whispered Melanie.

"Oh, hush!" Angeline hissed in return.

Charity squeezed Raina's hand. "You spend so much time with the lad, it is hard to imagine when he would be able to get into trouble."

Raina snorted. "Have ye *met* my son? Besides, I'm only with him part of the day."

"Yes, but that is more time than most mothers spend with their children these days."

Her friends were nodding along with Olive's assessment.

Sighing, Raina took Olive's hand in her free one, touched by the knowledge these women supported and loved her. "Thank ye. Although it's clear it's the hours each day I'm *no'* with him that he's getting into trouble. All this time I thought he was in the nursery with Annie, but clearly he's off being mischievous. What *is* his nurse doing when she's supposed to be watching over him?"

"Clearly *not* watching over him," said Melanie drily.

Before Angeline could come to her defense again,

Raina chuckled to show she agreed with her friend's assessment. "I suppose I'm going to have to take the woman to task and find out when he's been getting into this trouble—*thieving*—and why she's allowed it. For that matter, she might ken where all these things are going."

"See if you can find Dorset's hat!"

They all laughed at that.

"What?" asked Clementine, affronted. "He's still complaining about that stupid hat."

"Aye, we'll find the hat. And the spectacles, and those pillows..." Raina glanced around at her friends. "Perhaps ye can help me compile a list of the things he's filched over the last weeks?"

"Of course." Charity squeezed her hand again, comfortingly. "But not right now. Right now..." With a small grunt, she pulled Raina to her feet, and Olive followed as well. "Right now, we have to get you downstairs for your dance."

Groaning, Raina pulled her hands free and rubbed at her temples again. "The stupid dance, aye. I cannae believe Twit is making me dance with a blasted duke when I *should* be seeing to my son."

Chuckling at the unkind nickname for their favorite teacher, Melanie slid her arm around Raina's middle. "Well, if it's any consolation, you look just terrible."

Raina burst into laughter and rested her head against her friend's shoulder. "Aye, actually, it is. Thank ye."

"Anytime, dear."

One by one, her friends touched her hands or shoulders as they left the room, each showing her support and love silently. As they trooped down the hall and to the stairs, Raina allowed that love to buoy her and carry her along. Strangely, the revelation that Ewan was getting into trouble had been helpful; instead of dreading her foray into Society, she was busy thinking about the things which really mattered.

Her *son*.

Her son, whom she loved. Her son, whom she'd chosen when it came down to either being a mother or being in Society's good graces.

Five years ago, she'd been a young lady, newly graduated from finishing school, with stars in her eyes, and she'd fallen in love with a gentleman whom she thought loved her in return. It had taken strength to decline his suit, knowing what Society would think of her... But when others had urged her to have the babe in secret and give him away to a good family, she'd rejected that plan.

Ewan was worth more to her than all the balls and musicales and fancy dresses and dances with dukes at house parties.

The last few weeks, the time spent with him and Matthew and Cash, had been worth more than the disdain she was sure to experience tonight. Tonight, when she danced with the stiff, snobbish duke her friends had all described, she'd wrap herself in the memory of being in Cash's arms, and she'd be able to make it through.

After all, it was only one dance.

What could go wrong with only one dance?

CHAPTER 7

THIS COLLAR WAS STIFLING, but Cash shouldn't be surprised. He'd endured more than a few of these excruciating evenings since the Fangfoss house party had begun, each one more boring than the last. Not for the first time, he damned himself for agreeing to Matthew's demand to find a new wife.

He didn't *want* a new wife. He wanted Raina.

No. Thinking of her this evening will not help you.

Even though she was the one making him so miserable. If he hadn't spent the afternoon naked in her arms, showing her with his body exactly how much she'd come to mean to him, then perhaps this blasted formal attire wouldn't seem quite so confining.

The memory of her laugh, her smile...it was going to be all he could think of as he danced with whatever young miss the Countess of Fangfoss threw at him this evening.

Why in damnation had he agreed to this? Surely the

countess would understand if he bowed out one week and sent his regrets. Of course she would; the woman was almost comical in her attempts to impress him. She wanted the bragging rights associated with the local duke making a marriage match at *her* party.

But rather than encouraging him, this summer had taught Cash he didn't *want* one of the ladies at the Fangfoss party. He wanted a woman who could laugh easily and accepted his son as her own. One who made him want to forget his duties, rather than hide in them.

You're thinking of her again, aren't you?

Well, why not?

Grimacing, Cash resisted the urge to tug at his collar again and tried to focus on whatever his host was saying to the third man in their little group. Luckily, Dorset—Ambrose Montgomery, Marquess of Dorset—was offering up all the necessary responses, which covered Cash's abysmal lack of manners.

You're going to have to tell Matthew you don't want to marry.

That actually wasn't entirely true. The last month had just helped him remember what he *did* want in a companion, wife or not.

He should've asked Raina to be his mistress when he had the chance.

Tomorrow.

He'd meet her and Ewan at the river tomorrow, and he'd ask her then. He'd have his cook pack a special picnic —he'd learned over the weeks that Raina had a sweet tooth—and he'd wait until the lads were in the water, and he'd ask her then.

A reluctant smile tugged at his lips. Most men considered jewels and townhomes when planning to engage a new mistress, but here he was thinking of sweet cream and pastries and the summer sun.

But first, he had to get through this evening. Oh well. It wouldn't be the first time he'd danced one dance with a debutante then bid his farewells to the hostess, would it?

Honestly, not all of the young ladies were bores. There were a few that were too...*bubbly* for his tastes, which made him feel ancient. A few were pleasant enough but were far too interested in other male guests for Cash to assume they were actually interested in him, which bothered him not one whit. Now that he considered it, Dorset—the man he was supposed to be listening to, damnation—was currently engaged to one of those young ladies.

One lady had admitted an interest in travel, which would never do for a wife of his; duchess-hood notwithstanding, he had no intention of leaving Cashingham for any length of time, not even for London. Mother and Carlotta were ensconced in his London townhome, and he was happy here in York. He was a country duke and planned to stay that way.

One young lady, as he recalled, seemed to meet most of his criteria, but she hadn't seemed to care a bit about *him*. It had been a new experience to be dismissed as unimportant. His title alone made him interesting, so he'd never bothered to care what people thought of his personality.

Of course, that young lady had a bit of scandal attached to her name, but after consideration, Cash decided a scandal wouldn't bother him too much. It wasn't as if he left Yorkshire too frequently, and he agreed with Raina that most of Society had their heads stuck up their—

You're thinking of her again.

Blast!

It was likely bad form to be thinking of one's soon-to-be-doxy while impassively eyeing the buffet of marriage-minded young misses spread out on the dance floor.

I thought you decided not to marry?

Scowling once more, Cash didn't even bother to curtail his movement as he lifted his hand to rub at his temples. Did he care if his host thought him rude? No. He was often thought of as rude, but dukes were allowed to be rude.

"What do you say, Cashingham?"

Dorset's question, asked with a faint smirk, jerked Cash's attention back to the conversation, and let him know the other man knew he wasn't paying attention. Luckily, the marquess had better manners than he did; enough to take pity on Cash and re-frame the query.

"I was just commenting to Fangfoss that his wife has put together a stellar crop of young offerings, eh? And as near as I can tell, the house party has been a success."

"That's right," grunted the Earl of Fangfoss. "Almost all

the girls have found themselves fiancés, thank the good Lord. Perhaps this blasted party can finish sooner rather than later."

Although Cash didn't respond, Dorset chuckled dutifully. "Seeing as how I was lucky enough to be one of the first 'found fiancés,' I cannot say I complain. I will be forever grateful the countess put on such an affair."

"She's been talking about little else since we married," Fangfoss admitted. "The woman's sole goal, all those years of running that finishing school, was seeing her charges married off to the right men." He leaned closer and winked over the rim of his champagne flute. "Where *'the right men'* means men with funds and titles, of course."

"Of course," murmured Cash, his gaze sweeping the room, wondering how quickly he could make his excuses.

Dorset didn't seem to be in a hurry, however. Why should he, when the lovely young woman he was engaged to—that was her, over there in the red, chatting happily with the bespectacled wallflower, although Cash would be damned if he could recall either of their names—was sending Dorset flirtatious smiles?

"I am just pleased my Clementine had a reason not to go hunting for *'the right man'* before she found me," Dorset chuckled. "Although, as I understand it, all the young ladies here have reasons for not marrying."

Fangfoss harrumphed. "Some of them just claimed marriage didn't suit them, and some hadn't found the right chaps. There was a bit of a scandal for one of 'em, but she hasn't attended too many of Julia's *fêtes*, so I can't say much about her. My Julia's been at her wit's end with *that* one."

"I can imagine." Dorset was smirking, and Cash wondered if the man knew more than he was supposed to, thanks to his fiancée's gossip, or if he was just humoring the older man.

"I think that's the one you're supposed to dance with tonight, Cashingham."

Being addressed directly by the earl made Cash's eyes narrow as he tried to pick back through the previous minutes' conversation. Something about a scandal, wasn't it?

"Really?" he murmured noncommittally, then turned to place his almost-untouched flute on the tray of a passing footman. "How delightful."

While Dorset snorted quietly, Fangfoss turned toward the large double doors. "Julia told me the girl was being stubborn, but she'd force her to— Ah, here they are!"

Cash glanced once across the room at the gaggle of females who'd just entered. Gaggle? Herd? Flock?

A flock of women?

A swarm? A horde of women? A brood?

No, a *murder* of women.

Cash straightened, tugging on his waistcoat, although he knew he looked impeccable. Best to get this over with...

Slowly, as if his mind couldn't quite accept what his eyes had glimpsed, his gaze was dragged back across the ballroom to where the flock-gaggle-horde-murder was pulling a reluctant member toward him.

She was wearing orange, which really wasn't the most ideal color for a woman with hair her shade, was it?

Strangely, that was the only thought Cash's mind seemed capable of producing at that moment.

She was lovely, and she was wearing orange, which didn't make sense. No red-head should have the right to look lovely in orange, but she did. She looked lovely in that dress.

She looked even better *out* of that dress, Cash knew.

Hell, she looked remarkable in one of those ridiculous swimming costumes, and in a simple blouse and skirt, and in—

He blew out a breath, seeing the exact moment she looked up and realized who *he* was.

"Your Grace, may I present Lady Raina Prince, daughter of the Earl of Elephant." The Countess of Fangfoss became flustered, and leaned closer to her charge. "Is that right, dear? I confess I get all those Highland titles confused."

Still holding Cash's gaze, Raina murmured, "He's Laird *Oliphant*, but aye, an earl as well."

"Oh, excellent!" The older woman bustled back into position. "Raina, dearest, this is the Duke of Cashingham — *Blast*, no. I did that wrong, didn't I? Oh, do forgive me, Your Grace. You'd think I'd have this introduction business down after so many times, wouldn't you?" She clucked her tongue and shook her head, tugging Raina closer with her hold on the younger woman's arm. "Lady Raina, His Grace the Duke of Cashingham."

Would the woman ever cease prattling?

Judging from Raina's wide-eyed, slightly panicked stare, she was as surprised as he was at finally learning one another's full names and titles, and he decided to put them both out of their misery.

With a perfunctory bow, he murmured, "My lady," and offered her his arm.

As the countess bustled off happily to stand beside her husband, Raina carefully lifted her hand to rest against his forearm. Her touch was so slight, he barely felt it, and knew she was poised to flee. But even under her gloves, and the layers of fine wool he wore, he could feel her warmth.

Had felt her warmth. That very afternoon when she'd been wrapped around him.

When he'd been inside her.

The orchestra started, and of course, it was a waltz. It was never *not* a waltz, although to be fair, he suspected the countess planned it accordingly so he'd have the most time to spend touching her eligible young misses.

But Raina stood stiffly in his arms; her hand barely brushing his shoulder and her hazel gaze locked past his left ear. He could see the sparks in her eyes and knew she was angry.

As angry as he was shocked?

His movements mechanical, he began to dance. This was a far cry from a proper waltz, and Cash wouldn't be surprised if he began to trip over his own feet. Or her ridiculous gown.

It wasn't until after their first turn that she finally broke the silence, still not looking at him. *"Cashingham,"* she hissed accusingly.

And he understood her complaint. "If I were to have friends, they would call me Cash."

"No' Adolphus?" Her angry eyes flicked once to his, then away. "I assumed 'Cash' was yer last name."

"No." Normally, that would've been enough, but the need to explain himself to this woman, *any* woman, was a new sensation, and it dragged the explanation from his lips. "I told you it was part of my name."

Her reply was as stiff as his had been. "Aye, and a last name *Cassius* could understandably be shortened to Cash."

Ah. He remembered now, their first meeting, when she'd told him *Adolphus Cassius* was a truly terrible name. He'd agreed with her, but before he could ask her what made her think it was *his* name, she had nudged him with her shoulder.

And that casual touch had completely distracted him, making him think all sorts of delightfully improper thoughts. And completely distracting him from the entire name conversation, now that he thought about it.

They were still waltzing woodenly around the room, in an impression of a set of disinterested—and possibly broken—marionettes. Cash supposed the least he could do was make an attempt at correcting her misunderstanding.

"I'm Adolphus Merritt. My son is Matthew Merritt."

"*Merritt*," she repeated in a whisper, and then snorted softly. "A bloody *duke*."

"Cash is simply short for Cashingham." He didn't know what he was trying to do. Explain? Ease her pique? Defend himself? "My estate borders Fangfoss's."

"And the river? The oak?"

"On my property. I thought you knew."

She sniffed lightly, her gaze now resting on the hair above his temple. "I never bothered learning the local gentry, nor the name of the bloody duke Miss Julia was determined to throw at us."

Throw at *them*? He rather felt they'd been thrown at *him*.

Dear Lord, Raina was a *lady*. She was one of the countess's finishing school students—a *lady*. His brain kept circling back to that fact, apparently unable to come to terms with it. She was the daughter of an *earl*.

And only a few hours ago, his cock had been in her mouth.

Just the memory caused an improper stirring in his trousers, and he tightened his jaw to try to keep himself from revealing the way she affected him.

Why? You never cared before.

That's because "before" was just the two of them, or them and their sons, stretched out in the shade on a summer afternoon. Not waltzing mechanically around a ballroom for all to see.

She was a *lady*, and she'd been acting like a doxy. He'd been about to make her *his* doxy.

Damnation.

The rest of the waltz was just as rigid and awkward as the first moments, and Cash couldn't help but compare the woman in his arms now to the woman he'd held that afternoon. Although this dance barely counted, since she was doing everything in her power not to touch him, and he found himself disappointed by how stiff she was.

Even stiffer than him, if that were possible.

The thought did little to cheer him, and as soon as the musicians began their final flourish, he pulled her to a stop. Even though he stepped away from her, she was still staring resolutely at his left ear. Her cheeks were flushed —not with desire or excitement, he guessed, but with anger—but her breathing was measured, as if she were trying to maintain control.

She hadn't been trying to maintain control at The Sword and Sheath—

Stop it. It'll do no good to relive.

Despite his best intentions, he couldn't help but study the way her hair was swept up in some kind of fancy coiffure Amanda used to prefer. It made Raina seem very *ladylike*, very proper.

Not at all like the woman he'd come to appreciate.

He much preferred her with that glorious red hair down around her shoulders.

As if she could sense his thoughts, her angry gaze snapped to his, then away once more. "Yer Grace," she said rigidly, reaching for her skirts as if she might offer him a curtsey.

But he couldn't let her leave *now*. He couldn't walk away from this ballroom, from Fangfoss, as he'd intended. Not with all the things left unsaid between them.

"Lady Raina," he blurted, much too loudly. "Would you consent to a walk?"

He offered his arm before she could think of an excuse, and he saw her glance to the edge of the room where the earl and countess were watching. The older woman looked positively giddy with delight, and Cash assumed it was because he—as the duke—had never expressed an interest in any of her young ladies beyond the perfunctory dance.

But there was nothing perfunctory about this offer.

Too bad it wasn't the offer he'd *planned* on making.

Raina hesitated, then placed her hand atop his arm once more. And once more, her touch was as light as a butterfly's, making it clear she had no interest in physical contact with him.

She'd very much wanted physical contact before she'd known his full name, hadn't she?

"It's warm in here, isn't it?" he said blandly, planning to use that as an opening to invite her out to the garden.

Of course she understood.

"Aye," she agreed stiffly. "Yer Grace."

That title had been tacked on, almost flippantly, and reminded him of the way she'd screamed his name only a few hours before.

"A turn about the gardens, perhaps, my lady?" He tried to keep his tone mild, hoping she understood he wanted to go someplace private for the discussion they were sure to require.

"The gardens boast some interesting statuary." It wasn't exactly an agreement, but he took it as such.

"Shall I meet you there?"

"Why bother?" When he glanced at her, Raina's head was held high, her jaw tight. "Everyone here already thinks me a doxy. They'll assume I'm off for a private rendezvous with a handsome, eligible man, and—"

"Think less of you?" he murmured.

Her eyes flashed with surprise as she glanced at him, then away. "I doubt that is possible, Yer Grace."

Well, to hell with them. He was the bloody Duke of Cashingham, and tonight, he had the arm—and attention —of a beautiful woman. Let them say whatever the hell they wanted to say.

Head held high, he marched Raina right out of that ballroom, and he swore he felt her relax just the tiniest bit.

Until they stepped out onto the balcony.

She led the way toward the marble steps. "Miss Julia's gardens are this way."

The gardens. The perfect place for a private rendezvous with a very eligible young lady. Or, in this case, what Cash was certain would turn into a fight he wasn't sure he wanted to win.

He focused on her response. "Miss Julia?"

"Apologies." In the soft light from the ballroom

windows, he saw her roll her eyes. "Lady Fangfoss. The ex-Miss Julia Twittingham, founder of the Twittingham Academy." With a sigh, she folded her arms across her chest. "That's where we met. I was one of her Twits."

Cash's lips tugged at the irreverent name. "Our host briefly explained her efforts to see you all married."

"Aye, we were the misTwits, the unmarriageable ones." With a huff, she lifted her hands and began to tick off fingers as she spoke. "Clementine lost her fiancé right out of school, and was in mourning for five years until she met Dorset. Angeline returned to Ireland to nurse her ill father, and so didnae attend any of Society's fêtes to find a husband. Olive never had any intention of marrying, which was why—of course—I had to introduce her to my brother, Phin. They are absolutely perfect for one another."

Cash had settled on his heels, his hands clasped behind his back during her recitation. "The anthropologist?"

"Archaeologist," she corrected. "And Olive is just as obsessed as he is, bless her. Then there's Charity, who saw nae need to marry, when there was so much *fun* to be had." She ticked off her fifth finger. "Finally, there's Melanie, who is American and whose parents sent her here to snag a titled husband, but she's been much more interested in starting her own business."

As Raina wiggled all five fingers at him, almost in challenge, Cash cocked his head at her. He remembered all of those women, but... "Not *finally*. You forgot yourself."

With a huff, she tossed up her hands and turned away

from him. She *was* facing a statue—a classical rendering of a mother and child, which Cash thought was appropriate —but he doubted she was seeing it.

"And then there's me. I learned all about the pleasures of the flesh and chose to bear a son out of wedlock, therefore completely ruining me in the eyes of Society, which are—of course—the ones that matter." She said the words as if by rote, before whirling back around and piercing him with a dark glare. "I'm the most unmarriageable one of all."

She wasn't wrong. Even he had assumed the worst about her before he'd come to know her.

Of course, *after* he'd come to know her, he'd realized Raina was as perfectly unfettered and unconcerned as he'd hoped she'd be.

Lady *Raina Prince, you idiot.*

Something must've showed on his face, because she made a little noise of disgust and looked away. "Ye cannae even argue, *Yer Grace.*"

"What do you expect me to say?" he burst out, suddenly as angry as she. Angry at Raina for not telling him the whole truth, and angry at himself for not asking. For letting himself believe it didn't matter. "You are a *lady.*"

"Nay, I *was* a lady!" She snapped back, her hands falling to her hips. "Now I'm a doxy!"

The silence after her proud—bold—impossible— declaration fell hard, slamming around the inside of his head, echoing mockingly.

With a sigh, he reached up to rub at his temples, the irritation pounding behind them. "Your father is an earl."

"Aye, and my brother's a viscount. I have all the best education, all the best breeding, and I'm *still* ruined. Why? Because I had the audacity to—"

"Love your son," he finished quietly.

The reminder caused her to gape at him.

"Why are you so angry, Raina?"

"You're a *duke*, Yer *Grease*," she spat out. "Ye didnae think to mention that to me?"

He vowed not to be distracted by her attempt at insulting him.

"Well, *you're* a lady," he barked in return. "And you never mentioned it to me. I thought you—" He hesitated. "I thought titles didn't matter to you."

She threw an arm out scornfully, gesturing at him. "They seem to matter an awful lot to *ye*, *Dis*Grace."

He struggled to find his calm. "Are you trying to rile me?"

"Is it working?" she snapped. Then she threw up her hands and turned back to the statue. "Of course titles matter to ye— Ye're here searching for a wife, aye?"

So she remembered what he'd told her that afternoon, when they'd been basking in the aftermath of their ecstasy? "So what if I am?"

A small voice suddenly whispered in his mind: *An earl's daughter would be a suitable duchess.*

But not one who'd been so thoroughly ruined. Who'd allowed *him* to ruin her!

She scoffed as if she could hear his thoughts.

"Oh, ye'll get nae arguments from me! A minor country baron might be able to enjoy life, but a *duke* needs heirs, aye?" She turned just enough to glare over her shoulder at him, her hazel eyes spitting golden fire, and he couldn't recall ever wanting to kiss her more.

"I told you that," he barked in agreement. "But I thought you didn't care about titles." He thought she'd cared about—about *him*. As a man.

"Ye're the one who seems obsessed with titles, *Duke*! What does it matter who my father is?"

Because I can't make an earl's daughter my mistress, no matter how ruined she is!

And because she *was* ruined, he couldn't make her his wife.

Dukes did *not* marry their doxies.

"Because…" He swallowed, trying to make sense of this sense of loss. "Because what we've been doing is entirely inappropriate—"

"For an earl's daughter, but it was fine for a woman just looking to enjoy life?"

Which was what he thought her. Of course, that's what she thought of him as well.

With a growl, he threw up his hands. "I spent so much time *planning*." He stepped closer and lowered his voice. "I was going to seduce you with sweets and desserts and laughter and all the things I knew you liked."

"You didnae *have to*," she shot back, icily, as she slowly

turned to face him once more. But he saw the pain etched in her expression.

And that pain, the knowledge he'd somehow hurt her, although he didn't know how, caused his heart to thump in anger. Anger at himself.

"I can't believe I was going to ask you to be my mistress," he spat out in disgust.

Maybe it was his tone. Maybe it was his words.

Either way, Raina flinched, her chin coming up in the dim light as she stepped back. He saw her nostrils flex as if she were trying to calm herself, and his palms itched to reach for her, to pull her into his arms, to *apologize*, although he didn't know for what.

Finally, she sucked in a breath and haughtily turned away, holding herself regally as she strode toward the marble steps in that hideously wonderful orange gown.

But when she reached the top, she stopped, silhouetted in the lights coming from the large windows behind her. Her hand was on the banister as she turned to look over her shoulder, but he could only make out her profile in the light from the ballroom.

"I would've agreed, Cash."

She would've become his mistress.

Which is why she couldn't be his wife.

And then she was gone.

Damnation.

CHAPTER 8

I WOULD'VE AGREED, Cash.

It hadn't been an empty boast, but Raina couldn't stop thinking of her words to the man who'd broken her heart.

And aye, she knew having one's heart broken required one to be in love, and she was smart enough to admit that's exactly how she'd felt about Cash.

Excuse me, His Grace the Duke of Cashingham.

Cursing her own stupidity—and stubbornness—Raina kicked at a stone in the muddy path, sending it skittering along the edge of the otherwise finely manicured garden walk.

It had rained that morning and the air still held a feeling of heavy, damp potential. Overhead, the gray clouds swept across the sky, blown by a wind higher up than she could feel. Still, Raina tamped down a shiver she didn't quite feel and wrapped her arms around her waist as she walked.

Walked? Nay. She was sulking, and was bright enough to recognize it. At least none of her friends were there to tease her, and Ewan wasn't there to see that, sometimes, adults threw tantrums as well.

Her son had thrown a tantrum on Saturday, the morning after that disastrous ball. She'd gone up to the nursery to find Annie preparing him to leave with her for their daily outing to the river, and Raina had to sit her son down and explain they wouldn't be swimming in the river that day, or any other day.

He'd looked so confused, her heart had broken. Gathering him in her arms, she'd promised him, "We can swim in the river on Fangfoss property, sweetheart. Just the two of us."

That's when the poor lad had begun to wail, demanding Matthew. Knowing how close the two lads had become over the last weeks, her own tears had flowed. She was denying her son the first true friend he'd had, simply because she had quarreled with Matthew's father.

Nay, it was more than a quarrel. They'd realized, despite the act they'd been putting on all summer, there was no future for the two of them.

Love sought is good, but given unsought better.

Aye, she hadn't intended on falling in love with Cash, but somewhere along the way, it had happened. To her, he wasn't a cold imperious duke. He was a reserved man, aye, who had required some coaxing to emerge from his shell, but one who took the time to truly *be* with his son, who cared about *her* son in a way which surprised Raina, and who was gentle and loving and damned arousing.

But he was also a duke.

She sighed and tilted her head back to glare up at the clouds, refusing to allow the tears to form.

He was a *duke*.

Had he been just a simple landowner, or perhaps a baron, she would've felt free to engage in the physical relationship they'd started on Friday at The Sword and Sheath. She would've felt *free*.

I was going to ask you to be my mistress.

The word "mistress" implied being a kept woman, being beholden to one man, in exchange for gifts and securities. Raina still wasn't certain if she would've gone that far, despite what she'd boldly claimed to Cash. But the point was; the relationship would've been on *her* terms, because she knew she was his equal.

But no' when he's a bloody duke!

A duke could keep a mistress as long as he wanted. Raina wouldn't have been his equal, and while a part of her was so damned angry to find out the truth and have their gentle interlude destroyed, the rest of her was glad she'd found out his identity before she'd committed to anything.

I was going to ask you to be my mistress.

I would've agreed.

Oh, damn. Here came the tears.

Blinking rapidly, Raina turned toward the sound of the River Derwent and debated walking in that direction.

After the morning's rain, it would likely be churning heavily and flowing strongly, which matched her current mood.

However, the idea of going anywhere near the river made her chest tighten. Despite her promise to Ewan to take him swimming, just the two of them, she hadn't managed it in the days since that disastrous ball.

So many times, in the last few days, she'd been tempted to hike to the bend in the river where they'd met Cash —*the Duke of Cashingham*—and Matthew, just to *see*. Just to see if they'd been going swimming without Raina and her son. But what if they *were*? What if this separation hadn't affected them one whit?

Scowling, Raina turned back toward the manor.

Dinnae be silly, lass. He wouldnae be there. He's a duke, and he has responsibilities.

But what if he *was* there?

Huffing in irritation at her argumentative mind, Raina hiked up her skirts and stomped back toward Fangfoss Manor.

The butler saw her coming and opened the front door without even raising a brow at her muddy boots, although his gaze did flick meaningfully to the scraper. Smiling ruefully, Raina stopped to wipe the mud off as best she could before tracking it throughout the fine house.

This meant that she couldn't help but overhear the rather impassioned conversation coming from the private family parlor off the foyer.

"Oh, milady! *Please* forgive me! I don't know how it

happened! One minute it was there, and then I turned my back, and it was *gone!*" The plea ended on a wail, and there was the sound of someone else clucking a tongue.

"There, there, Cook. I'm certain it isn't as bad as all that." That was Miss Julia's voice, the countess. "What has gone missing this time? Hubert, are you paying attention?"

"Yes, dear." The sound of rustling newspaper told Raina the earl *wasn't* paying attention, not really. "Missing items, yes. I've heard rumors..."

"Oh, milady. I'm so sorry!" This was the cook again. "It's the trifle! For luncheon! The one you specifically requested because it's your favorite!"

Oh dear. Trifle was Raina's favorite as well.

The countess echoed her sentiments. "Oh dear! Well, this will not do! Hubert, it's one thing to have little items going missing, no harm done I'm sure, but an entire *trifle?*"

"One of the maids just got hungry, dear," the earl murmured.

The cook began to blubber again—half apology, half defending her staff—while the countess bemoaned the theft of her favorite dessert...and Raina blushed.

She had a fairly good idea what had happened to the trifle, and she needed to get up to the nursery to confirm her suspicion.

Straightening, she found the butler eyeing her boots, as if he knew she'd been lingering in order to eavesdrop, so she sent the older man a beatific smile and strolled toward the staircase at a leisurely pace.

Once out of the man's sight, however, she hiked up her skirts once more and quickened her pace. The nursery was on the third floor, and if she didn't miss her guess, that's where she'd find the missing trifle—with her mischievous son.

She was already calling his name as she stepped into the room. "Ewan? Lad, where are ye?"

The nursery appeared empty, and Raina frowned as she began to poke under tables and behind chairs, calling her son's name again.

There was a sound, and she straightened to see a surprised-looking Annie standing in the door which led to her small room.

"Lady Raina!" The young woman blinked in what seemed like genuine shock. "What are ye doing here?"

Wasn't it obvious? Raina's frown deepened. "I'm looking for my son. Where is he?"

The nurse's eyes widened as she glanced around. "He's no' with ye? I thought he was with ye! He's always with ye in the mornings—"

"No' today!" Raina cut her off as her hunt turned frantic. She tossed aside pillows and looked into the hearth, as if there was a chance Ewan was hiding inside it. "He was supposed to be with ye this morning, and now the trifle's missing, and *he's* missing, and—"

She suddenly straightened, pulling a pillow to her chest. Dear God in Heaven, what was the lad up to now?

Turning, she pierced the nurse with a stern look. The woman paused in her own search—really, what were the odds Ewan was hiding inside his own boots?—and eyed her worriedly. Raina hugged the pillow, then exhaled and straightened her shoulders.

"I've been meaning to talk to ye, Annie."

"About Ewan?" the nurse prompted hesitantly.

Raina nodded firmly. "I've been told Ewan has been getting into rather a lot of trouble at this house party." When the other woman opened her mouth to deny it, Raina hurried on. "Mischief mostly, but he's been *thieving* small items, Annie."

"No' Ewan—"

"Aye, my son is the culprit." Raina knew as well as any that her lad could get into mischief. "My friends ken him well, and confessed to me last Friday"—moments before that disastrous dance—"that the lad's been stealing small trinkets." As Annie gaped at her, Raina did her best to recall the list her friends had given her. "A hat, a handkerchief, Olive's spectacles, a least one book, numerous pillows, and a small painting."

"Milady," began Annie hesitantly, "I've no' seen those items." She looked around the room, her arms held out from her side. "Surely if he was thieving them, he'd bring them back here?" She went as far as to spin in a circle, looking around the room. "But I havenae seen anything new arrive in the nursery, no' like that."

Hmm.

Frowning, Raina looked around, admitting that, at first glance, she didn't see any of the pilfered items either. A stack of books might be hidden among the children's reading material, perhaps, but a new painting would stand out, as would the number of pillows which her son had filched.

And a pilfered trifle would *definitely* stand out!

With a groan, Raina sunk down onto one of the chairs, suddenly exhausted. A headache was building behind her eyes, and she *knew* it was because of the tears she hadn't fully shed that morning.

"Ewan is fine," she muttered to herself. She'd taught him how to be self-reliant, and knew he was just poking about the manor, likely trying to find someplace to hide the trifle he'd pinched.

Honestly, how in the world did a lad his age manage to steal an entire dessert? Was he just wandering around the manor at that moment, struggling to balance a giant crystal bowl of cream?

This will be messy.

Annie fell to her knees beside Raina. "Oh, milady! Please forgive me! All these times he was allegedly stealing these things—"

"No' allegedly," Raina corrected wearily. "I believe my friends. He's the culprit."

"But *when* would he do such a thing, milady? He's either with ye or with me at all times."

With a weary sigh, Raina dropped the pillow and began to massage her temples. "Apparently no'. *Apparently,* the wee rabble-rouser has figured out how to slip away with each of us assuming he's with the other. Like now, for instance."

The nurse was becoming flustered. "I swear, milady. I thought he was with ye. I thought ye'd taken him to the river to swim again—"

Raina lifted one hand to wave off her objections. "I should've had this talk with ye immediately after I learned of his shenanigans, but I was…distracted."

Distracted by a dance with a duke, and what she'd learned after that dance.

I was going to ask you to be my mistress.

I would've agreed.

Damnation!

"I'm sorry, Lady Raina," the nurse said quietly. "I understand if ye dinnae want me to work with Ewan after such a breach of trust—"

Raina waved away her objections with another sigh. "I'm as much to blame as ye are, for making assumptions. Let us find the lad, and together we'll explain how this is *no'* acceptable behavior. He's the one who set out to fool us both, and he deserves a punishment."

Annie offered a relieved smile. "Aye, milady. We'll put the fear of God in him!"

Nodding, Raina rose to her feet and offered a hand to her son's nurse. "Ye look up here, and perhaps in the servants' quarters, and I'll begin the search downstairs."

She might've said more, but a knock interrupted her.

They both turned to the nursery door as it opened and one of the footmen stuck in a head, looking relieved to have found her. "Lady Raina, you have a visitor downstairs."

Now? Who?

She wanted to snap out the question, but instead, she sighed and glanced at Annie. "Aye, and then I'll begin the search." She gestured to the footman. "Would ye please stay and help my son's nurse look for him? I'll be back as soon as possible."

The man was already agreeing as Raina hurried out of the nursery and down the stairs. Who would've sent a footman to fetch her? Her friends were already in the manor—unless they'd gone on some adventure and wanted her to join them? But then the footman wouldn't have called one of her friends—who were also guests—a *visitor*.

The explanation awaited her in the foyer.

Raina skidded to a stop on the upper landing, her skirts bunched in her hands, as she realized who waited for her inside the front door.

The Duke of Cashingham was waving off the butler's attempts to get him to wait in a parlor and was clutching a man's hat in front of him, while still wearing his own on his head.

He looked up and saw her. Raina would like to claim there were sparks between them when their eyes met, or something, and he *did* hesitate…but then he bounded up the stairs fast enough to cause her to step backward.

His expression… She'd never seen him like this. Almost frantic, if such a word could be applied to a man who normally kept himself strictly under control. Was he here for *her*?

He halted in front of her and waved the hat under her nose. "Tell me he's here," he barked out. "Oh God, Raina. Tell me he's here."

"Who?" She snatched the hat from him, turning it over in her hands. "Is this yers?"

"Matthew is missing."

It was the way he said the words, bleak and hopeless, that had her gaze darting back to his. The pain in his eyes caused her to catch her breath, and her lips formed the word "Matthew?" without any sound emerging.

Then his hands were on her upper arms, his grip strong. "Tell me he's here, Raina. Tell me he's run here to be with Ewan." His voice was harsh, full of pain.

"Did he miss Ewan as much as Ewan missed him?" Raina managed, her own tears pricking at the memory, and at the sight of this man's agony.

The man she loved.

The lads she loved.

"He was heartbroken when I told him we wouldn't be joining you at the river again." His grip tightened. "That was days ago, but this morning— *Oh God!*"

His voice cracked, and he hung his head, although he kept his hold on her as if it was the only thing that mattered. Instinctively, Raina dropped the hat by her side and lifted one hand to Cash's cheek.

"He's missing?" A suspicion curled through her mind, and her heart began to pound.

"Tell me he's here," Cash croaked.

It nearly broke her heart, but Raina had to shake her head, even knowing he couldn't see it.

"Matthew's no' here, Cash," she admitted, and before he could do more than suck in a breath, she continued, adding, "And Ewan is missing as well."

His head jerked up, piercing her with an intense, inquisitive stare. "He is? Are you—"

He broke off the question, and Raina ached to know what he'd intended to ask.

Instead though, he straightened, as if this news had revitalized him. "I was hoping Matthew was here, but afraid…" He shook his head, then jerked his chin at the hat she held, her other hand still cupping the side of his face. "I found that in the middle of the corridor outside his rooms. I was afraid it belonged to whoever had taken him."

Taken him?

Shocked, Raina lifted the hat once more to study it. It seemed ordinary, if fine. "Why would someone want to take…?"

"He's a duke's heir," Cash reminded her dully, releasing her arms and stepping away from her.

Raina dropped her chin. "Of course," she whispered.

Of course, he *was* a duke.

It was easier to study the hat than to look up at him, although she wasn't really *seeing* it.

"What are the odds both lads were taken?" she murmured.

"I wondered if they were together—"

"Oh, I say! That's my hat, isn't it?"

The new voice jerked Raina's attention upward once more, to find a grinning man hurrying toward them. It took a moment to recognize him as the Marquess of Dorset, Clementine's betrothed. The man was already reaching for the hat she held.

"Excellent show!" He beamed as he turned the hat over in his hands, his fingers checking the brim. "I've been looking for this for weeks, ever since that cheeky little lad ran off with it."

Raina's eyes were wide. "Ewan stole *this* hat? Ye're certain it was *this* hat?"

"Of course!" With a cocky grin, Dorset settled it atop his head. "It's my favorite hat. I wouldn't forget what it looked like. Damned fine, don't you think? Thank you very much!"

The man strolled off down the corridor, whistling merrily, as Raina turned wide-eyed to Cash. The man shook his head.

"*Dorset* took Matthew?"

"Nay!" She lunged for him, latching onto his arm in an attempt to get him to understand. "Ewan has been filching things from members of the house party. Dorset's hat, Melanie's cigarette case, books, a painting, a handkerchief..."

When he still didn't seem to understand, she shook him slightly, feeling the strength in the coiled muscles of his forearms.

"Do ye no' see? If Dorset's hat—which Ewan stole weeks ago—was outside Matthew's rooms…"

"Then Ewan must be at Cashingham," he finished in a whisper, his gaze on her lips.

"Aye, or somehow he's been passing his treasures to Matthew. The lads may be working together on this for some reason!"

"Is it possible?" he murmured, then shook his head. "Matthew said something to me recently about a fort—"

"Aye!" she interrupted excitedly, remembering a conversation with her son weeks ago. "Ewan said something similar. Is it possible they've been sneaking away to collude without either of us kenning?"

Heaven knew it wouldn't be the first time Ewan had escaped her care and his nurse's attention by making each think he was with the other.

She watched Cash's Adam's apple bob as he swallowed once, then twice. Finally, he nodded.

"Matthew has been heartbroken at the thought of not being allowed to see Ewan. I suspect you are correct, Lady Raina."

Lady Raina.

There'd been a time when he'd called her by her given name, and she'd called him Cash. But this was a reminder of what they were to one another now.

Just two concerned parents.

"Come along," she said softly. "Let us return to Cashingham. I've set the servants to searching for Ewan here—"

"And I for Matthew at home," he interrupted.

"Aye, but we ken Ewan's treasures are at Cashingham, and if the two have been meeting behind our backs, it is likely they are together."

He nodded, a harsh jerk of his head, and swallowed again as he pulled away from her touch. "Then let us hurry," he called as he trotted down the stairs toward the front door.

CHAPTER 9

His ride to Fangfoss Manor had been frantic and heart-pounding. Part of him had *known* Matthew had been taken, and the rest of him had been trying to drown out that certainty with the hope that his son had merely run away to be with his closest friend.

Now it appeared as if neither of those scenarios was true, and while he still didn't have answers, at least he was feeling calmer.

And that was completely due to the woman who currently had her arms wrapped around him.

His gelding had been waiting patiently for him beside Fangfoss Manor's front steps, and as he'd hurried out with Raina at his side, she'd surprised him by heading for the animal instead of for the stables, or ordering a carriage to be brought around. When Cash had hesitated, she'd cocked her head at him.

"This laddie looks strong enough to carry us both

swiftly, aye? Unless ye want to waste the time waiting for another to be saddled for me?"

It was the hint of challenge in her voice which convinced him. If she was going to doubt him—or his horse—then, by God, he'd show her!

But when he offered her his hand, and she swung up behind him and settled against him, her breasts pressed against his back and her arms looping around him, he wondered who the loser was in this scenario.

Certainly not him.

So, yes. This strange calmness which had settled over his shoulders, despite not knowing where Matthew was, was all thanks to Raina and the way her cheek was pressed against his back as the gelding galloped for Cashingham.

He was a *duke*, for God's sake, not some stable lad! He wasn't supposed to run pell-mell across his land, especially with a lady—an earl's daughter specifically—perched behind him wearing naught but a walking gown!

But on the other hand, he wasn't supposed to take time each day to go swimming with his heir and the woman who made him feel happy.

And he damn well wasn't supposed to fall in love with her.

But Cash was smart enough—and brave enough—to admit that's exactly what had happened.

He'd gone and fallen in love with Lady Raina Prince, and her adorable, invigorating, *frustrating* son.

Instead of alarm, the acceptance—because it was a

conclusion he'd been working toward over the last few days, ever since she'd left him alone in the garden last Friday eve—settled around him like a warm cloak, as comforting as her arms.

He loved Raina.

He loved her freedom, her informality, her *joy*. He loved the way she lived her life unapologetically, and he wanted to do that too, not just with her, but he wanted to be *part* of the life she lived. He wanted her in his bed, aye, but more than that.

He wanted to sit across from her at breakfast and argue about the latest edition of the *Times*. He wanted her on his arm, shocking all of Society with her outspoken support of worthy causes. He wanted her in his arms as they took their lads swimming and fishing and riding, and all the things normal, non-ducal fathers did with their children.

He wanted her to remind him how to be *Cash*, the man, instead of Cashingham, the duke.

But not Adolphus.

The thought had him smiling as he pulled the gelding to a stop in front of the portico at Cashingham, and when he swung her down, she noticed.

Her brow twitched upward. "Ye're looking pleased?"

He didn't release her hand. "I've come to a rather important realization."

Her expression softened, and she squeezed his hand. "That we'll find the lads? We will, ye ken. They're safe."

Her certainty made him accept this, even without knowing where Matthew and Ewan were.

"You're right," he murmured as he tugged her up the front steps. "They're in here somewhere. I'm just sorry..."

"What?" she prompted when he trailed off.

He pulled her to a stop before the grand entrance and exhaled as he tilted his head back to stare up at the grand edifice, which his forefathers had built to be imposing.

"This isn't how I'd imagined showing you Cashingham the first time," he said softly, his lips quirking ruefully.

"Och, aye? So ye had *plans*?"

"Raina," he sighed, finally meeting her eyes, "I had all sorts of plans."

"I remember."

I was going to ask you to be my mistress.

I would've agreed.

The words hammered in his memory, as they had so often over the last days. At first, he'd been certain her response had been the reason *why* he couldn't form any further connection with her. But now he was beginning to realize the challenge in those words—*I would've agreed*—were what made him love her.

Society would consider her the wrong kind of duchess.

But he didn't give a fig.

He loved her *because* she was the wrong kind of duchess.

No. She's exactly the right kind of duchess. For me.

Before he could say more, the front door swung open, his butler looking more than a little relieved. The older man stepped out of the way as Cash pulled Raina inside.

"Your Grace, I believe Mrs. Simms has found a new clue."

Cash nodded, the reminder of his son's current predicament dragging his attention away from future possibilities. He hoped the butler's announcement meant Raina's theory was correct, and the lads really *were* at Cashingham. "Upstairs?"

"Yes, Your Grace."

Your Grace. He was surrounded by people who knew him as the Duke of Cashingham, but Raina had called him, "*Yer Grease.*" The thought had him smiling as the pair of them hurried—her hand still in his—up the stairs.

"Your Grace!" His plump housekeeper waved as she hurried toward him. "Oh, Your Grace. Thank goodness—" She skidded to a stop and cocked her head at him. "Are you feeling well? Did you find the poor lad?"

He realized she was referring to his smile. Was he really that somber of a man?

He squeezed Raina's hand, knowing anyone who could call him *DisGrace* during an argument was someone who would always make him smile.

"We haven't found him, but we have some new clues. As do you, so I've been told?"

Mrs. Simms nodded hurriedly and thrust a hand into her apron pocket. When she pulled out what appeared to be a cigarette case, Raina made a relieved sound and dropped his hand to reach for it.

The housekeeper took a startled step back, but Raina snatched the case from her unresisting fingers. "This is Melanie's. I'm sure of it!"

Cash stepped up beside her to stare down at the colorful enameled case in her palm. "Melanie?" he murmured; his head bent until it almost touched hers.

"Miss Melanie Pennypacker," she elaborated, and Cash thought quickly.

"The American?" He'd danced with her several weeks ago, as he recalled, and she'd tried to press him into joining her in some kind of business venture.

A grin tugged at Raina's lips as she met his eyes. "Who else but Melanie would purchase a cigarette case enameled with a scene of a cowboy roping a steer?"

He allowed his fingertip to skim over the detailed scene. "It's very much something that would appeal to a curious young lad, is it not?"

If Ewan had been the one stealing all these little items, it was obvious why he'd taken this one.

Raina gave a relieved sigh before jerking her attention back to Mrs. Simms. "Where did ye find this?"

The housekeeper was glancing between the pair of them, as if startled to be addressed by a lady she hadn't been introduced to. But when Cash made no attempt to correct the situation, she blinked and pointed. "On—on the way up to the third floor."

The servants' quarters!

"Come," Cash barked.

Raina barely had time to slip the case into the pocket

of her dress before Cash took her hand and pulled her toward the small staircase at the end of the corridor.

Together, they thundered up the stairs, but at the top, Cash pulled to a stop. Here, the hallway was smaller and the doors closer together. Faces—maids and footmen, dragooned into the search—stopped to peer at him.

"Have you found anything else?" he almost shouted; sure they'd understand what he was referring to.

Heads were shaking in denial when one young maid spoke up from the other end of the corridor.

"Here, Your Grace." She lifted a pair of spectacles. "I found these—"

Raina pulled him down the corridor. "They dinnae belong to anyone here?"

The young maid tried to curtsey and hand Raina the spectacles all at once, and ended up tipping sideways before Cash righted her. It was obvious she was flustered over how odd it was for a strange lady like Raina to be wandering around the servants' quarters at Cashingham.

With the duke himself, for that matter.

Raina was peering at the spectacles, and the maid shook her head, attempting another curtsey. "No, milady, Your Grace. I asked, and no one recognizes them."

"I cannae be certain," Raina muttered, "but I believe these are Olive's. She mentioned Ewan filching a pair from her." She took a deep breath and looked up. "Show us where ye found these, and call off the hunt."

Cash's brows rose. "Explain," he demanded.

"Do ye no' see?" Raina rounded on him, waving the

spectacles as if they'd help make her point. "Ewan stole the cigarette case from Melanie, the hat from Dorset, and these spectacles from Olive!"

He reached for her, turning her to face him with his hands on her upper arms. "What does that have to do with the hunt for the lads?"

"If the pair of them are together, up to something..."

She blew out a breath and shook her head, and for the first time, he noticed her hair had come out of its simple coiffure sometime on the ride to his estate. No wonder the butler and housekeeper had stared at her in such surprise! But Cash didn't mind. He much preferred her looking like this to that ghastly, wonderful picture of a lady she'd presented at Friday's ball.

"Yes?" he prompted.

"If they're up to something, something to do with these things Ewan's been stealing, then these things were left for *us* to find. Matthew is a bright lad, Cash. He'd ken I'd be able to recognize the things Ewan has stolen."

His grip tightened briefly on her upper arm as he understood what she was saying, then softened as he exhaled. "You mean, our lads have set up an elaborate treasure hunt for *us*? We're supposed to follow the clues until we find them?"

Her smile was rueful as she nodded. "Does that no' sound like something they'd do? I'm sorry they put ye through such trouble."

He suspected she meant, *I'm sorry you had to come and*

find me, but he wasn't certain if that was because *she* didn't want anything to do with *him* anymore, or if…

God help him, going around in circles like this was going to give him a headache!

"Excuse me, milady?" The timid little maid spoke up, and when Cash and Raina turned, she shrank back. Swallowing, she asked, "Your—your son? Is he a young, tow-headed lad, perhaps four or five years old?"

As they both nodded in excitement, the maid glanced between them. "I've seen him with Lord Matthew several times playing up here. I—I thought he was a village lad, or belonged to one of the servants." Of course, someone as young and as new as this girl wouldn't know all the other servants' business as well as the housekeeper might. "When they see me, they duck out of sight, but I didn't think they were doing any harm, so I didn't tell—"

Since she was becoming emotional, Cash patted the air in an attempt to calm her. "It will be fine. I'm *glad* the pair of them have had time to play."

Raina huffed, which might've been a laugh. "And *I'm* pleased to ken where that naughty lad has been running off to! Do ye ken he's been allowing me to think he's with his nurse, while his nurse thinks he's with me? We had nae idea how often it's happened, but the lad's been coming *here*? All the way to Cashingham?"

He took her hand once more. "Matthew likely helped him."

"Och, aye." She rolled her eyes. "This also explains the

fort Ewan was going on about weeks ago. How long have they been planning this?"

The little maid was clearly lost. "Planning what, milady?"

Despite not having addressed the last question to her, Raina smiled at the girl. "What's yer name?"

"Millie, milady," the maid offered hesitantly.

"Well, Millie, it appears our lads have arranged a bit of a game for His Grace and myself."

As the girl's confused gaze swept between them, Cash nodded. "Sort of a treasure hunt." At least, he *hoped* that's all this was; a game set up by Matthew and Ewan to make their parents look for them. "And I'll tan that boy's backside when I—"

Raina clucked in exasperation, interrupting him. When he glanced at her, she smiled. "I dinnae think for one moment ye'd lay a hand on that lad in anger, Cash."

He grinned in return. "No harm in putting the fear of God into him though?"

She rolled her eyes and turned her attention once more to the maid who was staring, wide-eyed, at their banter. She'd likely never heard anyone refer to the Duke of Cashingham as "Cash."

Hell, she's likely never seen you smile either, you idiot.

"Can you tell us where you found these spectacles, Millie?" Before the maid could answer, Cash added, "And have Mrs. Simms call off the hunt." He squeezed Raina's hand without looking at her. "This is something for Lady Raina and myself, I suspect."

At the mention of Raina's title, Millie's eyes widened further, but she nodded and bobbed a curtsey at the same time. "At—at the end of the hall, Your Grace. I found them just lying in the middle of the rug."

When Cash nodded firmly, Millie's gaze dropped to their joined hands, and a faint smile tugged at her lips. He pulled Raina past the little maid; certain the story of their employer's madness would be all over the servants' dining hall by that evening.

Madness? Is that what love was?

Possibly, but he was surprised to discover he didn't mind.

Behind them, the hall quieted as Millie ushered everyone downstairs, and Cash was certain he could now hear his own heartbeat. Raina's fingers were entwined with his, in a way which somehow felt as intimate as what they'd shared at The Sword and Sheath last week. He glanced at her, and wasn't quite surprised to find her grinning.

Together, they pushed open doors and peeked in, trying not to disturb occupants if they were present. Most were small bedrooms belonging to the maids or footmen; some had one bed, some two, but each was cozy and comfortable.

But their sons weren't there.

Raina had resorted to calling out Ewan's name occasionally, but Cash didn't join her. If Matthew had wanted to show himself, he would've.

Her breath caught. "That one."

He wasn't sure what she was talking about until he followed her gaze to a door to what looked like another small bedroom. Unlike the rest of the rooms, this door was closed—mostly. There was a crack between the frame and the edge of the door, as if it had been closed in a hurry.

Or someone had done it on purpose.

They were already heading toward it, Cash's hand stretched out to push open the door—and hopefully catch their naughty sons—when a flash of white caught his eye. He glanced to the side.

There! Right in front of a small door—was that a linen closet?—a handkerchief lay crumpled. It was too careless to have belonged to the servants, but surely one of them would've noticed it.

He detoured, pulling Raina toward the piece of linen. She stooped and picked it up, dropping his hand in the process. Frowning, she bent over it.

"Do you recognize it?" he murmured.

"I dinnae ken." She rubbed the linen between her fingers. "Angeline told me Ewan filched a handkerchief from her fiancé—the Marquess of Rothbury—but I have nae way of kenning if *this* is it."

Humming, he eyed the small door in front of them. "It appears to be of fine quality." If it *did* belong to the marquess, then perhaps behind this door... "I wonder..."

He reached for the handle and pulled open the door to what he assumed was a closet.

He was wrong.

"Oh my..." breathed Raina as she slipped around him and stooped to enter what Cash could only call *The Fort*. It was remarkable.

"Look at all these pillows, Cash!" Raina had to remain stooped in the center of the space—it really wasn't too much bigger than a closet, and Cash suspected that's what it had been before their sons had taken it over. "I've wondered what in the world a set of lads would do with all the pillows Ewan was stealing."

Cash couldn't stop his chuckle as he leaned into the space, his neck craning around to peer at all the improvements. The floor, indeed, was strewn with pillows of all shapes and sizes, including more than a few he recognized from various parlors here at Cashingham. Had Matthew been filching pillows as well?

The original shelves had been removed from one wall to make more space—his son had found a set of tools somewhere, and Cash was surprised to realize how proud he was—but on the other side of The Fort, the shelves contained an eclectic collection of books. Everything from nursery stories to—he peered closer—Markham's illustrated *A History of Wheat, Volume Three*.

Hmm. Perhaps stolen by a lad who can't read?

He supposed he should be glad Ewan hadn't found volumes one and two.

His gaze skimmed over the books, rocks, and other assorted treasures the lads had stored on the shelves. There was a fishing hook—in honor of the time they'd spent fishing at the river?—and a perfectly round skipping stone. Propped against one shelf was a small portrait of Cash's mother, painted while in her youth, and a larger painting he didn't recognize. Had Ewan stolen a portrait from Fangfoss Manor to decorate their hideaway?

His breath caught when he saw the collection of wooden toys. Those soldiers Cash remembered as being Matthew's favorites as a younger lad. Had his son brought them from the nursery for Ewan to play with?

He closed his eyes on an exhale, his hands braced against his knees. *Dear God, lad. All you wanted was a brother, wasn't it?*

"Cash?" Amusement in Raina's voice drew his gaze back to her. "Look at this."

The space was cramped, but when she moved to one side, he saw what had been hidden behind her skirts. "Is that...a *trifle?*"

"Aye," she drawled, her hazel eyes sparkling with amusement. "Filched this morning from Fangfoss Manor, if I dinnae miss my guess."

A trifle? Ewan had stolen the messiest kind of dessert he could pick and had carried it to Cashingham?

"*Why?*" he asked, shuffling further into the small space.

"Because, I suspect, it's my favorite."

It was the note of laughter in her voice which snapped his gaze back to hers, and suddenly, he was remembering his plan to ask her to become his mistress. He'd planned to seduce her with strawberries and crème and enough sweets to make her say *aye.* But the thought of her licking her spoon clean after enjoying the trifle...?

Well, it was an entirely inappropriate time for a cock-stand, but that didn't seem to matter one whit to his body.

Blast.

And then her lips curled upward, as if she knew what he was thinking, and he took a step toward her. "Raina—"

That was as far as he got before a weight barreled into his backside, sending him stumbling forward. Luckily, she caught him before they could both go headfirst into the trifle, which was perched on a wobbly little table, but when he tried to turn, he cracked his head against the low ceiling.

"Ow! What the devil?" Rubbing his head, he turned to see the door was now closed. When he tried the handle, he wasn't at all surprised to discover it was locked.

And a glance at Raina told him he'd get no help from her. She currently had her hand pressed against her lips to keep from laughing.

"It was Ewan," she whispered, her eyes sparkling. "I saw him pull the door shut."

It was more likely Matthew had done the kicking, while Ewan had locked them in, and Cash was surprised by the burst of pride at the realization the pair worked so well together. Still, he needed to teach these lads they couldn't trick their parents this way.

Stepping up to the door, he placed his fists on his hips —the impressiveness of which was marred, he could admit, by the fact he had to hunch over—and bellowed, *"Ewan Prince, you open this door immediately!"*

Silence from the other side of the door met his demand.

But then, to his surprise, she stepped up beside him. "Matthew Adolphus Roger Merritt! Yer father and I are verra disappointed, young man."

Cash's brows crept toward his hairline. When had she learned Matthew's full name?

Although he could see the twinkle of amusement in her eyes, she'd made her voice sound stern. She knew exactly how to deal with their wayward offspring, and something swelled in Cash's heart as he saw further evidence of how good a mother she was.

God help him, but she was *magnificent.*

From the other side of the door, he could hear frantic whispering, but he only caught a few phrases. "How did she—" and "…middle names mean you're in *trouble!*" Then there were some hushed exchanges, and a few scrambling noises, then silence.

He exchanged a questioning glance with Raina, but she just shrugged. They both leaned slightly toward the door, wondering if their gambit would pay off.

Finally, he heard Matthew clear his throat. "I'm sorry, ma'am. But we both think it's necessary."

Cash hadn't expected to be affected by hearing his son's voice clearly for the first time, especially after they'd figured out the boys' scheme. But after the last few hours of worry and frantic searching, his knees went weak. Since he was already bent almost double, he just accepted the inevitable and dropped to one knee.

"Matthew, lad, are you and Ewan safe?"

His son responded immediately. "Yes, Da—I mean, Father." *Da* was Ewan's word. Had Matthew been spending so much time with the younger lad, he'd begun to speak like him? "But we needed to get the two of you together. To talk."

Cash became aware that Raina had sunk to her knees on the pillows beside him, her fingers pressed against the door. He turned to watch as she slowly rested back against the pillows, her eyes wide, as if she could stare *through* the door.

Without tearing his gaze from her, Cash called out, "And Ewan's there with you, Matthew? He's safe too?"

To his surprise, the younger lad piped up in answer. "We're both safe, Father. I stole the trifle because it's Mama's favorite, and so you wouldn't starve, even if you're in there forever and ever because she's stubborn—that's what Uncle Phin says—and you have to remind her she loves you, that's what Matthew says, Father."

Father.

Ewan called him "father." *Twice.*

And Cash's heartbeat had sped up at hearing it both times.

That's what you want.

Until today, he hadn't realized *that's what he wanted*. He *wanted* the mischievous, devilish little lad to call him Father. He wanted Matthew to be able to call Ewan brother.

Cash's breath caught. He wanted Matthew to be able to call Raina "Mama."

He realized he was staring wide-eyed at her, which was making her flustered. She dropped her gaze to her lap and waved a hand too dismissively to be convincing.

"He just heard Matthew say it," she managed.

"Yes."

Father.

She risked a peek up at him. "The me-loving-you-thing, I mean."

He took a moment to really look into her eyes and saw the hesitation and concern there.

"Do you?" he murmured.

She dropped her gaze to her lap. "My feelings arenae a concern here."

He disagreed. But… "*I* was speaking of the fact your son called me Father."

"Oh!" Her head jerked up quickly enough to smack against the shelf behind her, but she didn't flinch. "He just heard Matthew say that, as well. He's verra young, remember."

Smiling wryly, Cash reached for her hand. As he enfolded it in both of his, he settled down on his arse on the pillows beside her. "He's not so young he can't master-mind a series of daring thefts to furnish this fabulous hideaway *and* drop a series of clues for us to follow."

Her lips twitched, but her gaze remained on their joined hands.

"I'm certain it was Matthew who was the mastermind

behind *that* hunt." Before he could object and point out his heir was mild-mannered and bookish, she lifted one shoulder in a half-shrug. "Ewan only called ye Father because Matthew calls ye that. No' because he thinks *ye're* his father."

"No, his father was an abusive bastard whose nose I'd like to break." The words popped out before Cash could think better of them.

Raina's gaze jerked up to his in surprise. She stared at him for a few moments, before finally saying softly, "Which is why I willnae tell ye his name."

Maybe not now, but one day…

Cash vowed he'd do what he could to help her get the revenge she deserved. *If* that's what she wanted.

An unexpected smile tugged at his lips as he held her gaze. Speaking in a normal tone, without looking away from her, he spoke to the door. "Lads, can you hear me?"

"Yes, Father," they chorused almost in unison, Ewan's little voice half a beat behind Matthew's.

His smile grew at the sound, and her brows dipped in confusion.

"Go away for ten minutes."

She blinked at him, and from the other side of the door, Matthew asked, "Ten minutes?"

"Yes, lad. If I can have ten minutes alone with Raina, I don't think we'll have to be in here forever and ever." That had been what Ewan had threatened after all.

Her eyes had widened again, and there was a bout of hurried whispering on the other side of the door. When

Cash heard Ewan hiss, "That means there'll be trifle left-over!" his smile grew. Then, Matthew said very clearly, "Come along, Ewan. They want some privacy."

There followed the sound of footsteps, and Cash cocked his head to one side, listening to make sure they were really gone. Meanwhile, Raina was staring at him, her hand rigid in his, while her other hand gripped her skirt in her lap.

His smile softened as he understood the signs of her worry. She wasn't sure what to expect from him, and he couldn't blame her. He'd been so angry—mainly at himself —when he'd discovered she was an earl's daughter because it meant he couldn't have her in his life the way he wanted...as his doxy.

But maybe he could have her in his life the way she deserved.

As Matthew's mother. As his wife.

Thinking of the way she jumped to discipline Matthew, and the sparkle in her eyes when she'd done it, he asked softly, "You love him, don't you?"

He remembered the way she'd gently taught him new things beside the river, how she effortlessly touched him as if he were a normal boy, and how gentle she was with him. She *did* love him.

But the question flustered her further, and she dropped her gaze once more. "Ewan? Of course I love him."

"No, not Ewan," he corrected gently, releasing one

hand to raise her chin so he could study her hazel eyes. "Matthew. You love them both."

She flushed, but because of his touch, she couldn't look away.

"You love them both," Cash repeated in a whisper. "And they both love you. Matthew loves you."

I *love you.*

His throat closed up.

She was blinking rapidly, and when he realized there were tears in her eyes, he released her so she could look away.

He cleared his throat, deciding to change the subject before she lost control of those tears. "Will you tell me who Ewan's father is?"

She blinked, and her eyes jerked back up. Frowning, she gave a quick shake of her head before her gaze skittered away again.

Taking a deep breath, Cash reached for her other hand. Sitting there, in their sons' secret hideaway, reclining on pillows stolen from a dozen different rooms and two different homes, he squeezed both of her hands and smiled.

"Will you tell me who Ewan's father is on our first wedding anniversary?"

CHAPTER 10

WHAT?

The faint pattern on the silk of her skirts suddenly jumped into sharp focus as Raina studied it. Flowers, she thought, or something equally feminine. It was unlikely to be a bundle of phalluses, although that's what they looked like to her at that moment.

Focus, lass.

She *was* focusing, that was the problem, but on the wrong thing.

Her pulse was loud in her ears as she slowly dragged her gaze away from her gown—which was likely irrevocably ruined since her morning sulk outdoors, her frantic ride clinging to the Duke of Cashingham, and squatting here in a closet—to the man who'd just asked such a ridiculous question.

Will you tell me who Ewan's father is on our first wedding anniversary?

Cash was sitting there, holding her hands, staring into her eyes as though it was the most natural thing in the world, and she wanted to check him for head injuries. Hadn't he bumped his head when the boys had pushed him in here? Maybe he had a concussion.

But he was still staring at her as if expecting an answer, so she managed a strangled, "What?"

"Will you tell me who Ewan's father is—"

Before he could get to that wonderful, impossible second part of his question, she interrupted him with another firm shake of her head. "Nay, Yer Grace. I'll no' tell ye his name."

"Cash," he corrected gently, squeezing her hand. "And why not?"

Why not? She frowned, trying to find words to make him understand. "He...doesnae matter. No' anymore. He was an arsehole, aye, but an honorable one. He didnae ruin my life—it was *my* choice to deny his suit and turn my back on Society. And I dinnae consider that such a ruin, to be honest."

"He was cruel to you," Cash pointed out.

"Aye, he was cruel to everyone. I see that now. But he's married and has three little ones, whom he ignores. His wife seems happy enough with her new title, and I suppose is willing to put up with his temper."

"If he's married, all the more reason to ensure he's punished for his cruelty."

She shook her head in frustration. "Do ye no' see? He's nothing to me, no' him or his family. He doesnae claim

Ewan and has never hinted of our past connection. That's good enough for me to leave him be."

Her pulse had slowed, and she found herself leaning toward him, almost pleading with Cash to understand.

"I dinnae want to think about him, Cash."

"What he did to you—"

"Was nae different from what ye did to me," she snapped. And as soon as the words left her mouth, she gasped, realizing too late what she'd said. Straightening, she tried to convince herself to apologize, to explain she hadn't meant it, that Cash meant more to her than any other man possibly could, and she loved him.

But it was too late. The words were said, and he'd winced, acknowledging the barb.

Sitting back, Cash slowly released her hands. For lack of something better to do with them, Raina twined her fingers in her lap and dropped her chin, watching him from under lowered lashes.

He blew out a breath and dragged a hand through his hair. Now it was disheveled, the way he'd looked after swimming with her at the river. Last Friday, when she'd looked across the ballroom and seen the composed Duke of Cashingham as her next dance partner, she'd barely recognized him in his icy perfection.

But this man…? This man she *knew*.

"So…are you going to just ignore the fact I proposed marriage?" he finally said.

So had Ewan's father. But nay, she couldn't stand to compare the two of them.

"Is that what ye were doing?" She tried to keep her tone light. Without looking at him, she aimlessly picked at the pattern of probably-not-a-bouquet-of-phalluses on her gown. "I thought it was a duke-ly command."

"It's *ducal*," he corrected, "and I don't want to command you."

"Ye could." It took a moment to realize the whisper had come from *her*.

Peeking at him from under her lashes, she saw him shake his head in frustration. But she was right; he was a *duke*, for God's sake, and she'd already been in his bed once before. Although they weren't formal, Society would already consider her his doxy.

But...*marriage?*

"I don't want to command you," he repeated.

Then, to her surprise, he lunged forward, scooping up her hand in both of his again.

"I don't want to command you, Raina, because that's not who I am. And it's damn certain not who you are."

Her lips formed the word, "What?" as she finally lifted her chin, but no sound came out.

"You are strong and brave and smart, Raina. You don't take the easy path when you know it's not the right one. You do what's best for you and Ewan, despite knowing how hard it will be, and you've weathered everything Society could throw at you, and *you still have love in your heart*." He squeezed her hand, his blue gaze intent. "So much love, Raina. I don't want to command you to do anything. I want to *ask*, to beg even. I want to be the right path for you. I want you to choose me because it's the right thing for you and Ewan."

Before she could even begin to process his words, much less think of an answer, his shoulders slumped slightly.

"I want you to love me," he whispered.

It was the plea she heard in Cash's voice which broke her heart all over again. Hearing him say such wonderful, perfect things to her, caused her resolve to weaken. She'd thought her heart couldn't hurt any more than when she'd had to accept they couldn't be together, but now...

Tears gathered in her eyes as she covered their joined hands with her second one and squeezed his knuckles. "I'm sorry, Cash," she whispered. "I learned long ago that loving someone wasnae a good enough reason to spend my life with them."

Her heart had been wrong about Ewan's father, and she had been lucky enough to realize her mistake in time.

To her surprise, he blinked at her for a moment, then snorted in derision. "That's a stupid thing for someone as smart as you to say." Before she could object to the insult, he shook his head. "Loving someone is the *best* reason to spend your life with them."

This was harder than she'd expected, and she'd never expected it to be easy. Not that she had ever expected him to offer marriage in the first place.

When she closed her eyes, she felt twin tears leak out from under her lids and couldn't call them back. She *knew* she was making the right decision for herself, but did that mean she was making the right decision for Ewan? For Matthew? *For Cash?*

She swallowed, then whispered in a small voice, "No' if they dinnae love me in return."

"Is that it?" The question burst out of him with an exhalation which might've been a laugh...or incredulity. She opened her eyes to see him staring at her, one corner of his lips pulled up as he gazed fondly at her. "Have you *really* not realized what I'm trying to say? I take it back, Raina. You're brave and strong, but sometimes, you're very silly."

She blinked at the insult, her shoulders slowly straightening as she tried to figure out his meaning. "I may no' be the smartest woman, but—"

"I love you."

She frowned at the interruption. "No ye dinnae." He was just saying what he thought she wanted to hear, after her confession. "Ye want a mistress. Someone to warm ye at night."

He clucked his tongue, then sighed, almost ruefully. As if he were...*disappointed*? Disappointed in her?

"Remember what you once told me?" Cash's lips quirked as he mimicked her brogue. *"If a woman ever found herself lucky enough to be loved by ye, she should insist on marrying ye."*

She'd said that?

Aye, she'd said that.

But...is that what he was saying? She was lucky enough to be loved by him?

Raina sat in confusion as he shifted awkwardly in the tight space, moving pillows out of the way and cursing under his breath, until he finally settled down next to her. She watched him warily, unsure what he was going to do next, as he leaned back, muttered something, and straightened far enough to reach for a pillow.

It was the pillow Ewan had stolen from the parlor at Fangfoss, and Cash shoved it behind his back with a little sigh. Then, to her surprise, he reached around her, pushing against her shoulder, until she had no choice but to rest against him.

Truthfully, it wasn't a hardship. She *wanted* to be in his arms again, had yearned for little else these past days without him. It had been so very hard to have a taste of paradise in his bed, only to have it stolen away by cruel fate and their positions.

But now...

"I want you in my bed, yes," he finally said, his low voice rumbling through the small space and through the chest she was resting against. "I've never made a secret of that, and I loved that you didn't hide your attraction to me, not even at the beginning."

"Desire," she corrected quietly.

"Hmm?"

"I desired ye. It's more than just an attraction."

She heard the smile in his voice, although she didn't glance up to see it, when he agreed,

"Yes. And I've never met a woman I desired more than you, Raina. You're beautiful, aye, but strong and brave and

—well, all those things I said. Funny, and loving, and *fun* to be around. You make me want to be with you." When he swallowed, she felt his throat move. "I like the man I am when I'm with you."

She sighed, her palm pressed against his chest, and her fingers playing with his waistcoat. "A mistress could…"

She wasn't sure what she'd been trying to say, and when she trailed off, she felt him shake his head.

"A mistress could warm my bed and make me happy, but I wouldn't hold her heart. That's what I want, Raina. I want you to love me as much as I love you. I want…" His hand closed around hers, where it rested against his chest. "I want you in my bed, yes, but I also want you at my breakfast table. I want to read the newspaper with you and argue about coal prices or mining practices or the latest translation of Homer or—or any of the thousands of things you have opinions about."

Suddenly, he sat up, dragging her with him and turning her until he could grasp her upper arms and stare into her eyes. "I want to raise our sons together. I want to stroll into church with you on my arm, looking magnificent, with them behind us, whispering up shenanigans when we're not looking. I want to take them swimming and fishing and riding *with you*. I want you to help make Cashingham a *home*, not just a house, Raina." His grip tightened as his voice rose. "I want you to make this *your* home. I want you to have the chance to snub society and Ewan's father as a *duchess*. I want you to have access to whatever resources for charitable works you'd like, even

though I know you'd rather be with our sons, loving them.
I want…"

All the fight seemed to go out of him, and he slumped,
his hands falling from her arms to rest against her hands
in her lap.

His chin dropped, and he muttered, "I want *you*, Raina
Prince. I want to spend the rest of my life loving you."

It was…

That was…

Raina gaped at him.

That had been the most perfect speech she'd ever
heard—could ever have imagined hearing. It was so
perfect, her brain couldn't seem to make sense of it, and so
it latched onto one of the last things he'd said.

Numbly, she realized her mouth was moving. "I've
always thought it would be nice to have an organization
to help other women who were left in my situation, so
they didn't have to make a choice they'd regret later in
life."

Seriously? Of everything she could've said, *that's* what
came out?

But he didn't seem to mind. When he lifted his face, his
eyes were full of hope.

"Then do it," he whispered, squeezing her hands gently.
"Duchesses can do anything."

Just like dukes. Her lips quirked. "I dinnae like Society."

That was an understatement.

"Neither do I." His reply was immediate. "I'd be
content to stay here in the country, traveling only to

London on occasion when duty—or my mother—demands." He hesitated. "However, we might have to host the occasional house party."

She frowned, hating the idea of inviting Society into her home—was she already thinking of Cashingham as her home? Nay!—to gawk at her. "What kind of house parties?"

His lips curled upward. "The kind of parties where you invite your school friends every summer for a reunion."

Damnation. He knew the way to her heart.

He knew her heart.

She blinked and straightened.

Cash knew her heart.

Wide-eyed, she realized she was already leaning toward him. "Ye really do love me, Cash?"

"With all my heart." His voice softened as his fingers rose to caress her cheek. "These last days, without you…" He shook his head ruefully. "I believe I was in love with you before that afternoon at the inn, you know. But when I learned who you really were, I stubbornly pushed you aside, believing I knew the way things should be. But I realize now I was being just as judgmental as Society has always been. I *love you*, Raina Prince, and I want to keep on loving you for the rest of my life. Not as my mistress, or some other temporary arrangement. I want you to stand up in front of your friends and family and swear that you'll be mine forever."

Oh.

Oh dear. She was crying, wasn't she?

Although he'd gone all blurry, Raina was able to lift her hand to cup his cheek. "And ye'll be mine forever?"

She saw him smile. "Is that a yes?"

Instead of answering—not sure she could form the words—she tugged him closer, and he came willingly. When his lips closed over hers, it was like coming home. He tasted of mint and her tears, and something undefinable. Familiar. Perfect.

He tasted of *forever*.

With a little groan of need, he pulled her closer, sliding her onto his lap. She went willingly, twining her arms around his neck and failing in her attempt to retain a smidge of awareness. They were sitting in their sons' fort, for God's sake, and any minute—

His hand closed around her breast, hidden beneath her corset, and she moaned as all objections fled her mind. Instinctively, her pelvis arched against his hardness, as if meeting an old friend, and the desire she felt for him, which always flickered not far beneath the surface, burst into flames.

As his lips traveled across her jaw to that sensitive spot beneath her ear, Raina tilted her head back with a sigh. Her eyes were closed, and she accepted the truth.

She loved this man.

She loved this man, and she trusted him enough to spend a lifetime loving him.

"Raina," he whispered against her skin, his breath causing her to shiver. "Raina, love…"

"Aye," she groaned, her fingers twining in the hairs at

the base of his skull, and her knees falling open instinctively. "*Please*."

His grip shifted, moving her in his lap until his hardness pressed against her hip, and his other hand cupped her arse. She was prepared to attempt to make love to him in this cramped space—

The knock on the door had them both jerk in surprise.

Cash slammed the back of his head against the shelf again, then muttered a curse. "What?" he barked, as Raina did her best to regain control of her breathing.

The knocker hesitated, then spoke. "Father? Ma'am?"

"Matthew," Raina whispered, meeting Cash's eyes in time to see him wince.

Had it been ten minutes?

Her entire life had changed in only ten minutes.

Dinnae be stupid. Ye've loved him for far longer.

Aye, but she didn't know *he* loved *her*.

With a sigh, Cash began to set her gown to rights. "I don't suppose we could plan an assignation to continue this later?" he whispered to her with a naughty wink.

Delighted, she squirmed against his arousal. "I believe I could find time to sneak away to The Sword and Sheath again."

They were both trying to keep their voices low.

His forehead dropped to hers as he exhaled. "I was thinking more of prevailing upon my neighbor—dare I call him friend? Likely not—the Earl of Fangfoss, for a more permanent invitation to his wife's house party."

Raina's eyes widened at his solution. He was willing to

come stay at Fangfoss Manor, even for a few days, in order to bring them closer together?

"Perhaps that would work, Yer Grace. The guest room next to mine happens to be available, I ken. And I also ken there's room for Matthew in the nursery with Ewan, should ye choose to break with all tradition, and bring yer son to the house party. It'll likely shock the countess slightly less than me declaring my intention to bring my bastard son."

When he chuckled, his warm breath washed over her, calming her heartbeat. "I would like that. And perhaps, once duty calls me back home, you might visit me?"

"Here at Cashingham?" The idea of being so blatant about their desire sent a spark of excitement through her.

"And beside the river." He smiled crookedly. "I find I prefer being Cash and Raina to being the Duke of Cashingham and his..." His gaze flicked over her as his smile grew. "Lady Love."

She was about to respond, to tell him she much preferred him as a man than a duke, when the pounding came at the door again.

"Mama! Did ye spank him?"

When Cash's gaze grew speculative, and he raised a challenging brow, Raina had to smirk and look away.

"Not too horribly, son," Cash called out, his voice as even as he could make it, despite the laughter she heard lurking. "I believe I'll survive."

There were more whispers, and then the lock *snicked*.

Raina was trying to push herself off his lap when the

door was yanked open, and she froze, realizing she'd look more guilty for trying to change positions.

When Matthew's gaze landed on her, with his father's arms still around her, and his brows went up, Ewan stepped into the tight space, his gaze landing on far more important things.

"There's still trifle left, Matthew! Good thing we got extra spoons!" Beaming, he plopped himself down on a pillow beside Raina—and the trifle—and reached into his pocket for a big spoon. "I didnae want to leave spoons at all, because I think trifle's more fun to eat with yer hands, but Matthew said we had to leave some for ye." He waved the spoon enthusiastically enough that Raina ducked away from it. "So I nicked us some spoons so we could eat some too!"

Smiling, Raina reached for his hand, trying to calm the frantic motions in the tight space. "I think that's a lovely idea, Ewan. Far better than trying to eat with our hands."

"I told him that's unhygienic," Matthew intoned, sinking to his knees on the pile of pillows, and eyeing the trifle speculatively himself.

"Did you tell him he also need not steal our spoons?" Cash asked, laughter in his voice.

When Matthew sighed and nodded, Raina could very much see the resemblance to his sire. "He says it's more fun to filch things than ask permission."

"I suppose that would explain this room?" Cash asked.

Matthew glanced at Ewan, then met his father's gaze

firmly. Since Raina was still sitting in Cash's lap, she was met with the lad's seriousness head-on.

"I'm sorry for filching things, Father," Matthew said, his shoulders back, accepting his faults like a little gentleman. "It *was* Ewan's idea, but I—I *liked* it. I've never had a fort before, and it sounded so grand when he proposed it, and…and I wanted to have fun."

He dropped his chin, and Raina felt Cash's sigh against the back of her neck. She knew what he was thinking, because she was thinking it as well.

"Oh, Matthew." She slid from Cash's lap, but instead of moving beside him, reached instead for his son's hands. It resulted in her lying half-across the man she loved, half-reclined on a set of pillows, but staring into Matthew's serious gaze.

"Lad, yer father loves ye more than ye can ken, and he wants ye to be happy. And if having a secret fort is going to make ye happy, then he wants ye to have a secret fort. Ewan is too wild, and ye are too serious, but together, ye play perfectly. Ye each temper the other, and ye're both better for it."

Just like her and Cash.

Matthew ducked his chin, although he kept his gaze on her. "Not very much a secret anymore, is it?" he asked shyly. When she hummed in confusion, he explained, "You and Father know about our fort now."

And all the servants who helped follow the clues they'd left out, but she wasn't going to say that.

Fortunately, Cash replied instead. "I think it can still be

a secret fort, as long as the only people who know about it are the ones who love you."

Matthew's blue gaze, so like his father's, swept from Cash to Raina and back again. "And you love us? Both of you, love both of us?"

Raina nodded as Cash said, "Of course we do, lad."

When Matthew turned to her, Raina smiled. "Aye, Matthew. Yer father has shown me that I *do* love ye, as much as I love Ewan."

"And..." Matthew glanced at Ewan, then back to her. "And him? You love Father, don't you?"

Raina's grin grew, and she squeezed the lad's hands. "Aye, Matthew. I love yer father. And he loves me."

Ewan's whoop startled them all, and when he threw up his spoon in excitement, he knocked against the shelves, causing the portrait of the regal lady in blue to wobble. "I *told* ye it would work! They just had to talk! Can we eat now?"

Before she could answer, her son dug his spoon into the bowl of trifle, emerging with a helping far bigger than his mouth. Still, that didn't stop him from trying to eat it, and she lunged for him—"Ewan!"—and missed.

Now she was lying on her stomach on the pillows, and as her son stuck the spoon in his mouth and most of his serving landed on his cheeks and shirt, she began to laugh.

Behind her, Cash chuckled as well, and she dragged herself upright to sit beside Ewan and the small table with the large, ruined trifle.

"I cannae believe ye carried an entire trifle from Fang-foss," she admitted with a shake of her head.

Ewan swallowed and beamed proudly, covered in crème and pudding. "I had to, because it's yer favorite." It *was* her favorite, and the fact he'd stolen it for her was exasperatingly sweet. "It was also my idea to use the things from Fangfoss that couldnae go in the fort as clues for ye!"

That was a convoluted sentence, but Raina squinted thoughtfully. "Ye mean the things ye couldnae use to decorate this place? Like Dorset's hat and Olive's spectacles?"

Ewan was already digging into the trifle again as he nodded enthusiastically. "Uh-huh. But I lost the billiard ball. Sorry."

With a sigh, Raina pinched the bridge of her nose. She was going to have a serious talk with Ewan about his stealing—even if, in his mind, it was for a good cause—but perhaps not now, when she was sitting on the stolen pillows, watching him eat stolen trifle.

The trifle *did* look rather tasty, despite being a bit travel-worn.

Only a few feet from her, Cash had pinned his heir with a serious stare. "I can't condone the theft, son, but Raina is right. I'm pleased you and Ewan have made a place for yourselves."

Matthew ducked his head and smiled shyly. "It was my idea to find a way to get you together."

"Yes, and while I appreciate the outcome, the

method…" Cash blew out a breath as he shook his head. "Son, I pray you'll never know the level of fear I experienced when I couldn't find you. I was so afraid something terrible had happened."

He was using vague terms, but Matthew responded to the sadness he heard in his father's voice by leaning forward and planting his hands on his knees, as if the intensity would help. "Father, I didn't mean to make you afraid. I'm sorry! I just thought that if you and—and—" He glanced at Raina, obviously not sure what to call her. "If you and *Ma'am* had to work together to look for us, you'd realize how sad you've each been, and…"

He trailed off, dropping his chin and sitting back on his haunches once more. "I'm sorry," he repeated in a whisper.

Raina exchanged a glance with Cash and could tell he was wavering as much as she was.

"Matthew," she said softly, reaching for the lad's hand, "what ye did…it scared yer father and me. It was done with the best of intentions, and it worked, for we've had our discussion and realized what we want for the future, but it was scary no' to ken where our children were."

The lad squeezed her hand, his big blue eyes full of sorrow. "I'm sorry for hurting you, ma'am."

There'd been a moment when he'd called her *Mama*. She offered him a kind smile. "I'm willing to forgive ye, but please ken that yer father and I are relying on ye to temper Ewan's impulsive tendencies." With her other hand, she ruffled her son's hair, trying to keep her sleeve out of the crème smeared on his face as he licked his spoon. "In the future, I'm certain we'll allow the pair of ye freedom to roam, but we'll be relying on *ye* to ensure yer brother's safety, and we have to ken we can trust ye."

Matthew sucked in a breath, his eyes widening further. "Brother?" his whispered, his gaze darting between her and his father.

Cash's lips quirked upward. "Does that mean you'll marry me, Raina?"

Taking a deep breath, she offered him her future. "Aye. I will." Because now she knew he loved her, and that was all it would take for her to be happy for the rest of her years. "But I'll no' give ye the name."

"I'll ask you again on our first anniversary."

She smirked. "Ye're welcome to ask."

To her surprise, Cash chuckled. "I suspect that being married to you will be an adventure, love."

An adventure?

Her expression softened, and even though she wasn't sitting beside him, she tried to show him her affection when she smiled at him. "I'm going to make certain the pair of us, and our lads, have the most comfortable, most fun family."

"Fun!" piped up Ewan, his mouth full.

He'd already more than halfway decimated the trifle, and she still hadn't had any!

As she reached for the spoon, Cash sent Matthew a mock-stern look. "Look at this boisterous lad. At least *one* of our sons is serious and studious enough to temper his impulsiveness."

Raina kept herself from moaning as the pudding and crème passed her lips, but she must've made some noise, because Cash's eyes flew to hers, and the heat burning in them left her no doubt what he was thinking about when his gaze dropped to her lips.

Hopefully, he'd take a room at Fangfoss Manor that very evening!

"Father..." Matthew cleared his throat as he reached nonchalantly for one of the spoons. "I hate to tell you this, but I suspect I'm not having quite the effect on Ewan as you and—and *Mama* hope."

The name was said with a bit of relish, and she and Cash shared a smile as the lad dipped his spoon into the trifle.

Perhaps it wasn't a good idea to become so distracted, because Matthew straightened up, his spoon full of trifle. "You see, rather than me making Ewan more serious, he's taught me how to have *fun*."

With that, Matthew flicked his spoon, sending the blob of trifle across the intervening distance to splat across his sire's cheek and chin.

Cash froze, Raina gasped, and Ewan burst into peals of laughter. A heartbeat later, with Cash still blinking in shock, she had to press her lips together to hold in her own chuckles. In a flash, she'd turned back to the trifle, dipping her own spoon into the gooey mess.

As Ewan doubled over with laughter, clutching his

middle, Raina turned back to Matthew. "Lad, I love yer father, and as such, am loyal to him. I love ye as well, but I must defend him."

With that, she flicked her spoon, sending the blob of trifle to splat against his chest. Matthew gasped, Ewan's laughter redoubled, and Cash growled, "Hand me that spoon."

The four of them froze, then burst into motion. In a moment, trifle was flying this way and that, until they were all gooey messes, and the fort wasn't much better. More than a little managed to land in Raina's mouth—it was delicious—and she herself landed in Cash's lap.

He was delicious as well.

And through it all...there was much laughter. She was surrounded by the people she loved, who loved her, and she knew, no matter what the future might bring, she'd ensure it also brought even more laughter.

EPILOGUE

THE SCREAMS and yelling had long since faded to tears of wonder, and now there was silence.

Cash lay in his grand bed—the one he'd shared with Raina these last twelve months, the one the maids had just finished fussing over—and stared down at his wife and newborn son.

Although the midwife had objected, he'd insisted on being at her side throughout the entire ordeal. After all, a year with Raina as his duchess had taught him doing what was expected wasn't always doing what was right. The charity she'd started to help unmarried mothers find safe work and childcare for their children, was growing in popularity, and his own investments had grown since she'd introduced him to her friends' husbands.

No, what was expected wasn't always the right thing, and Raina had taught him the path to happiness lay in standing up for what you knew was right.

And although it had been the most terrifying, disgust-ingly wonderful few hours of his life, Cash had known, in this case, doing what was right meant being by Raina's side.

"You did it, love," he whispered, one fingertip caressing the infant's soft cheek where he suckled, half-asleep, at Raina's breast.

She sent him an exhausted, indulgent smile. "I cannae believe ye insisted on staying."

"*I* can't believe how strong your grip is," he teased in return. "I thought you were going to twist my hand right off."

"And *I* thought ye were going to cry when I started blaming my pain on ye!"

Cash winced as he shifted positions, making sure his arm, which he'd thrown around the pillows behind her head, wasn't catching her unbound hair. He vowed, as long as he lived, he would never forget the sight of her in her now-pristine nightgown and gorgeous red hair spilling around her shoulders, as she nursed their new son.

"Thank you for going through that," he whispered fervently, his hand moving to cup the babe's dark head. "Thank you for giving us another son."

When he looked up, he saw the tears in her eyes as she gazed at him. Over the months of her pregnancy, he'd become used to his normally so-sure-of-herself wife's mood swings, and he still hated to see her cry. This time though, she was smiling through her tears.

"Are ye certain ye're no' disappointed in another lad?"

Cash had made no secret of his desire for a daughter, but he scoffed. "How could I be? Ewan and Matthew have another brother now. I suspect we'll have to set up guards to ensure they don't steal the babe from his cradle and carry him off to indoctrinate him in some kind of adventure. Besides, I'll just insist on a girl for the next one."

As her grin turned to a good-natured grimace, Cash reconsidered. "Although if you never want me to touch you again as you claimed, I do understand."

She chuckled lightly as she lifted her knees and removed the infant from her breast. He made a pitiful little mewling noise, his lips still working adorably, as she laid him against her thighs so they could stare down at him.

Raina nudged Cash with her shoulder. "Ye ken I love yer body, husband, and how ye can make me feel. But I think it'll be a few months before I remember that, aye?"

"Aye," he agreed with a chuckle, pulling his arm closer to her shoulder, and reaching out to stroke his new son's open palm. The babe's fingers tightened around his digit, and he smiled. "His hair is darker than I expected."

"Mine was dark when I was a wee bairn," she was quick to point out.

"Oh good." He shot her a grin. "I was hoping for a little red-head."

"He's going to be just as mischievous as Ewan, is he no'?"

Cash couldn't seem to stop grinning. "And just as

thoughtful as Matthew. The best of both of our lads in one."

The new parents subsided into silence for another minute, studying the way the infant waved his hands about, almost in frustration. Cash tilted his head so it nudged her temple, and he felt her relax against him.

"Raina?"

She hummed softly, and he knew she was tired.

"Do you know what today is?"

He saw her blink, then nod. "Our first anniversary."

Smart lass. "So? Will you tell me the name of Ewan's real father?"

She straightened in surprise, her eyes widening, as she turned slightly toward him. He saw the moment she remembered the question he'd asked her, that day while they were locked in their sons' secret fort.

In the weeks leading up to their wedding—apparently, no matter what his wishes, a duke wasn't allowed to hurry his own wedding—and in the year since, he hadn't asked her again.

"Oh, Cash," she whispered, her gaze softening. "Aye, I'll tell ye."

Even though he'd asked, he still hadn't expected her to agree. "Really?"

Raina's hand rose to cup his cheek, an awkward movement with the babe lying between them against her legs.

"*Ye*, Adolphus Merritt. *Ye* are Ewan's real father."

His throat closed up, and he knew she was right, as always. The man who had sired Ewan could never love him a fraction of how much Cash loved the lad. *He* was the one who'd taught Ewan how to ride his pony. *He* was the one the lad came to when he fell and needed a hug. *He* was the one who sat in the nursery each evening and read nursery tales to his younger son, as Matthew studied his own books.

Cash *was* Ewan's real father, in the only way that mattered. *Love.*

"Thank you," he whispered again, staring deep into his wife's eyes. He captured her hand and pulled it toward his lips to press a kiss against her palm. "Thank you for giving me two more wonderful sons, Raina."

"Oh, Cash." Her eyes were clouding with tears again. "I love ye so much."

"And I love you." He settled her back against the pillows, this time, holding her more tightly. He cleared his throat and turned his attention back to the little lad on her lap. "Now, what about this young gentleman? What shall we call him?"

She was silent for a moment, stroking the babe's cheek, before she inhaled, and said, "I was thinking...Julian? Julian Prince Merritt."

"Julian." It took him a moment to place why that name was important. "After the Countess of Fangfoss?"

"The former Miss Julia Twittingham," Raina whispered. She glanced at him with a hesitant smile. "If no' for her, I would've never come to York. If no' for her house party, and her insistence I dance with a stuffy old duke..."

"And if you hadn't taken Ewan out for daily swims to

thwart her efforts, we would've never met," he finished with a smile. "But the stuffy old duke didn't turn out to be so bad, did he?"

"Och, aye," she disagreed, with a great roll of her eyes. "The *duke* is boring. Now, the *man*…well, him I fell in love with."

Chuckling, he tightened his hold on her and pressed a kiss to her temple. "I love you, Raina Oliphant Prince Merritt."

She rested her temple against him. "And I love ye," she whispered.

At that moment, there was a light knock on the door, and without waiting to be invited, it cracked open.

Two small, beloved faces peered around the edge. When they saw their parents lying in bed—awake and staring at them—the lads straightened up.

"The baby!" whooped Ewan, then attempted to launch himself across the room toward the bed.

But thank goodness his brother was faster.

Matthew reached Ewan before he'd gone more than a few steps and wrapped his arm around his younger brother's shoulders. "*Shush*! You must be calm and gentle."

Together, the pair of them approached the bed at a more sedate pace, with identical expressions of wonder on their faces. There were tears in Raina's eyes, but she was smiling hugely, so Cash didn't think the lads noticed; thank goodness, because the last few months had shown they hated it as much as their father did when Mama cried!

He helped her sit up and shift over, so Ewan—who was clutching a wooden soldier in one fist—could climb up beside her. He snuggled up next to her as Matthew squeezed against him, both of them staring down at the baby in awe.

"It's so tiny," murmured Matthew.

"Can it play yet?" Ewan waved the soldier. "Is it a lassie?"

Smiling through her tears, Raina gently propped the babe higher on her thighs. Cash reached around to support the infant's head, and at that moment, his new son opened his eyes.

Logically, Cash knew the lad couldn't see anything much past his nose, but he felt as if the infant was staring right into his soul. This babe, this tiny human he'd created with Raina...he would bind their family together, tying them together tighter than any knot.

And Adolphus Merritt, the Duke of Cashingham, fell in love all over again.

"Lads," whispered Raina to their sons, "I'd like ye to meet Julian Prince Merritt, yer new brother."

As Ewan and Matthew exclaimed in delight, and Raina showed them how to gently touch the infant's hair and stroke his palm, Cash rested against the pillows and watched his family, his heart more full of love than he ever thought possible.

He knew the coming years might contain hardships and heartbreak, but as long as he was surrounded by this same love and joy, he could face anything.

Raina's hand found his, even as she spoke to their sons. She squeezed it, and he squeezed it in return, and he knew this love would sustain him.

Forever.

BONUS EPILOGUE

FIVE YEARS LATER

Raina sighed happily as she sat back against the settee in Cashingham's front parlor. This room was one of the larger entertaining spaces the estate boasted, but it wasn't her favorite. She much preferred the more intimate room in the rear of the house, beside Cash's study, where she responded to correspondence and dealt with the details of her various organizations.

However, over the last few years, it had become apparent that this parlor was the only one which could hold their growing horde.

Oh, not that her and Cash's family was all that large: The two of them, plus Matthew, Ewan, Julian, Charles, and now, sweet Victoria, who was doing her best to pull up on her mama's lap so she might chew on the ear bobs Raina wore.

But when she looked around the parlor, at her friends and their gathered family, "horde" really *was* the only applicable description.

The summer after the Fangfoss house party, Raina had taken her husband's suggestion and hosted a gathering of her five closest friends and their families. In the years since then, each summer, they'd gathered as able. Oh, there was the one year Angeline and Rothbury couldn't attend because their son had decided to arrive early, and the summer Olive and Phineas had chosen to spend in St. Petersburg on request from the tsar's Minister of History…but they all cherished the opportunity to see each other once a year when they could.

Little Victoria yanked extra hard on her ear lobe, and Raina winced. "Nay, darling. Ye ken yer mama doesnae like that."

Chuckling, Olive joined her on the settee, her eyes sparkling behind her spectacles. "She's a curious little thing, isn't she?"

"Too curious," Raina admitted with a sigh. "With four aulder brothers, I worry what mischief she's going to get into."

Now that Matthew was away at school for part of the year, Ewan was reveling in being the eldest of their own little horde, and while his older brother had tempered his shenanigans a bit, he had in turn taught Julian and Charles to be quite the little terrors.

But Olive just scoffed and leaned over to tweak the bairn's nose. "They're going to get her into mischief, aye, but they'll also get her *out* of it quickly enough." Raina smiled to hear her sister-in-law speaking with a hint of Phineas's and her own Scottish brogue. "Is she ready to walk yet?"

"Almost." To demonstrate, Raina lifted her daughter from her lap and bent to place her on the floor. Victoria immediately pulled herself up, using her mama's skirts, and stood on her own for a moment, before plopping down on her padded rear end.

Raina and Olive chuckled as the bairn lost no time to crawl toward the group of youngsters gathered near the cold hearth, where Cash and Ewan had brought down some of the toys from the nursery. Angeline's youngest son was playing there with Melanie's lad, and it looked as if one of Clementine's twin daughters was directing them all. Her older son, Augustus, was part of the group of unruly youngsters which included Charity's wee James, as well as Angeline's older son. The whole boisterous pack were being led by Raina's lads in what appeared to be a reenactment of the Battle of Hastings, judging from the wooden swords and tin helmets.

"I'm looking forward to spending more time with her at Christmas," Olive said shyly.

Raina, who'd been smiling as she watched her husband chatting amicably with Phineas, the Marquess of Roth-bury, and Frank Crymble, slowly turned to her sister-in-law. "But…" She pursed her lips thoughtfully. "Ye usually spend the winter months abroad at one of your Mediter-ranean dig sites."

It was something about the way Olive glanced down, her fingertips brushing against her stomach, which offered Raina an explanation, and she gasped. "Olive!" She grabbed her friend's hand. "Really?"

Her brother and his wife had spent the last five years gallivanting around the globe, having the sorts of adventures Raina could only imagine. They hadn't seemed interested in starting a family, and frankly, they didn't seem to have time for one.

But Olive was glowing happily, and she nodded with a smile as she squeezed Raina's hand. "It's time. I'm not getting any younger, and we think we should be able to take off just this one season. Phineas can use the time to properly catalog his own collection and catch up on investments. And then, next winter, when the bairn is weaned, we can take him or her with us to whatever dig site we're assigned to next."

Unable to help herself, Raina leaned over to hug her sister-in-law and close friend. "I'm so happy for ye," she whispered against Olive's coiffure, thrilled by the strength of the return hug. "Ye and Phin are going to be wonderful parents, and ye'll give this little one an education my bairns will envy!"

Chuckling, Olive straightened. "You're welcome to send any of them along with us. We can teach them all sorts of things—" Her eyes widened. "Except maybe not Ewan. Not for a few more years."

Raina had to laugh at her friend's expression, realizing the trouble Ewan could get into at an archaeological dig.

"Och, I cannae even bear to send the lad away to school, how could I send him to North Africa?" She sent a mock glare. "Now, ye might want to offer to take Charity's Louise; I ken she's a handful!"

They both turned to watch their friend, who was seated with Melanie, trying to pick something out of her daughter's hair. A stick? A bug? Oh dear.

At that moment, Angeline came bounding over; a huge smile plastered on her face as she reached down to pull Raina to her feet. It was amazing how, in the years since their time at Twittingham Academy, dear Angeline still managed to retain her enthusiasm for life.

In fact, all Angeline wanted was Raina on her feet so she could give her a hug, apparently. Raina happily returned it. "What's this about?"

"I'm just so *happy* to be here! We all are!" Angeline enthused, her hand dropping to cradle her rounded stomach. "Clementine and I were just saying how wonderful it is that you host us each year, allowing us the opportunity to see one another. Rothbury and I adore the chance to catch up with all of you!"

Raina glanced at Angeline's husband, who was still chatting with the group of gentlemen. Frank had broken away to speak with Dorset and Wilton, Charity's husband, but Rothbury was still speaking solemnly to Phin and Cash.

"I dinnae think I can imagine Rothbury *thrilled* about anything."

Giggling, Angeline poked her. "Don't let his serious mien fool you. He's a big squishy softy."

"I don't think I want to hear this," murmured Olive.

Clementine, who strolled over with one of her bairns on her hip—Raina still couldn't tell the difference between Lily and Violet, to her shame—nodded seriously. "I don't need my daughters hearing about squishy man-bits."

"Thank goodness Charity dinnae hear that," Raina replied, smirking, "or we'd have to hear jokes about all *sorts* of things."

"No," giggled Angeline again. "Now that little Louise is turning into as much of a hoyden as Charity used to be, she's trying to pretend to be proper to set a good example."

There was a pause as they all considered that unlikelihood, and then they all burst into laughter.

That was when Melanie and Charity chose to join them, and Olive stood, until the six of them formed a tight group.

"What's so funny?" Melanie demanded.

Instead of explaining, Raina changed the topic. "We were discussing our planned shopping excursion to Crymble's the next time we're in London. I only buy my underthings from ye, ye ken."

"Oh, Lord," muttered Olive, "we're talking about *underthings* instead?"

But Melanie, who could always be counted on to discuss her department store, launched into an explanation of how she and Frank planned to expand in the next year. She and Clementine began a discussion about expected fashion trends in the coming year; since Clementine had started her own matchmaking business for gently bred ladies, helping them find love, she did her best to stay abreast of the latest trends. Her husband, Dorset, was content to stay at their home of Tildon Court, renovating as necessary and supervising their growing family.

Charity snaked her arm around Raina, and the pair stood in happy silence for a long moment. The two of them had been the least marriageable of the lot of them, but Raina knew they were both explicably happy. Although they only saw one another during the summers, Charity wrote to her often. That's how Raina knew her dear friend had recently taken up painting, despite her lack of talent back in her finishing school days. Raina was trying to commission her friend to paint a Venus to hang in Cashingham's library, but Charity had thus far refused.

But Raina was confident she'd wear her friend down, and was already holding a space for the future painting. It was, incidentally, right by the shelf where the place of honor was held by the first printing of Viscount Wilton's book of puns. Anyone who'd spent any time around Charity's husband understood the man's use of puns to keep his mind ordered, and her group of friends were all exceedingly proud that the man had published them, even if more than a few were groan-inducing.

Angeline tilted her head against Raina's other shoulder and sighed happily. "Who would've thought so much joy could've come from that summer at Second Chance Manor? I was only looking forward to a few weeks with my closest friends to recover from my father's death, but we all found so much more, didn't we?"

Slowly, Raina turned to frown down at her friend. "What did you call it? Second Chance Manor?"

Who understood how Angeline's brain worked, especially now that she was pregnant again?

But her friend blinked and straightened, as the other conversations trailed off and the five other women faced her. "Oh. Well, that's what I call it to Rothbury, that summer at Fangfoss. Are the earl and countess joining us for dinner again this evening? I so enjoyed meeting their little boy. He's adorable!"

"Focus, Angeline," Olive said in exasperation. "We're asking about your name for Fangfoss Manor."

"Oh, Second Chance Manor!" Angeline beamed and cradled her stomach. "Well, why not? It *was* a second chance, for me anyway. I missed out on so much, since I had to leave England immediately after school to return to nurse my father. When Miss Julia—"

"*Lady Fangfoss*," her friends corrected in a chorus.

"When *Lady Fangfoss* invited me to her house party, she was really giving me a second chance at finding happiness."

Some of the others looked doubtful, but Clementine shrugged. "It was most definitely a second chance for me. I lost Walter so soon after we left school and assumed I'd never find love again. Meeting Dorset—being forced into an engagement with him—was the second chance I needed. Now I can help others find that same love."

Olive looked doubtful. "I suppose I could agree that it was my second chance as well, although I didn't really have a first chance, did I? I thought I was happy being a wallflower, living my life in the library, but meeting Phineas reminded me of my dreams to travel, and together we have all sorts of adventures."

When her hand dropped to her stomach as well, Raina knew her sister-in-law was thinking about her *next* adventure: Motherhood would be unlike any of her exploits thus far!

Charity had removed her arm from Raina's waist, and now dropped her hands to her hips. "Well, I *know* that summer was a second chance for me, because I was able to overcome the scandal that was chasing me. Thanks to Wilton, I realized I didn't have to flee England to find happiness, *and* I learned the truth about my mother."

As everyone nodded, Melanie spoke up. "I don't know about *second* chance. I'd had so many chances to follow my dreams—and failed each time—I might say that summer was my *last* chance. But it worked, and not only did I find my Frank, and happiness, but I finally managed to fulfill my dream with his help."

Well, that was impossible to deny, certainly. Raina reached out and took Charity's hand, and Olive's as well. Olive reached for Melanie's hand.

As Clementine used her free hand to grasp Angeline's, and Angeline took Melanie's, Raina smiled. "Well, nae one can doubt that house party was *my* second chance. No' just my second chance to see all of ye, my dearest friends again." She squeezed the hands she was holding. "I'd made my choices, and although the consequences werenae easy, I didnae regret it. But that summer..." Shaking her head, her gaze traveled across the room to find Cash, who was smiling at her. "I found a happiness I didnae think possible."

Angeline beamed. "See? Second Chance Manor is appropriate."

Her friends murmured in agreement. Raina glanced around the unbroken circle, six women who had faced and overcome so much, and smiled at them, her sisters.

"Second Chance Manor, indeed."

Don't worry: The story continues in *The Duke's Virgin Sister*! Check out this romp of a romance between Cash's hoydenish little sister and a thoroughly unsuitable prizefighter...full of laughs and naughty bits!

AUTHOR'S NOTE
On Historical Inaccuracy

After reading such a story as this one, I'm sure you'll agree that *clearly,* the most important thing to discuss is Victorian bathing costumes. This is a long and boring history of fabrics, styles, cuts, and Victorian morality which—

Holy hell, even *I* can't manage that with a straight face.

You know how we all have this idea of uptight Victorian morality? There's lot of amusing anecdotes: Victorians invented bed skirts so they wouldn't have to look at a set carved legs (for fear of engendering arousal among those sexually attracted to wooden posts, I've always assumed). And they started referring to poultry bits as dark meat and light meat, so they wouldn't be forced to discuss "legs" and "breasts" in mixed company.

Which, of course, leads to even more interesting extrapolation about Victorian poultry-based kink.

Hey, if you're into turkey breasts in that way, we don't kink-shame around here.

Okay, the whole point of me bringing up these anecdotes is to point out that, if someone were to base their impression of Victorian morality on the pamphlets and sermons of the day, we'd have no choice but to assume these people were buttoned-up prudes.

But...I mean...why in the hell do you think those morality pamphlets existed? They were preaching what the author thought life *should* be like, not what it *was* like. The reason the sermons were so clear about what was necessary to live a good life (prayer, abstinence, bushy mustaches, regular ear-canal cleaning, whatever) was because life *wasn't* like that. Our Victorian ancestors weren't stuck-up prudes intent on leeching all the enjoyment of wooden table legs out of life. Trust me. They enjoyed doing all the naughty things *you* enjoy doing, you weirdo.

I am, of course, talking about laying around eating chocolate, reading books...generally enjoying life. I dunno what *you* thought I meant.

Now, onto bathing costumes. Because, while I just got done telling you these people weren't killjoys, they *did* invent going for swims in black wool, and while I'm sure there are worse things than that, I can't think of anything right at this moment. Hot needles under my fingernails, maybe?

Wait, to be fair, their ancestors *did* swim in yellow canvas, which filled with water and billowed out, rather than clinging to the wearer's body and showing their general—*gasp!*—shape.

But anyhow, the Victorian era was when we started to see advances in bathing costumes. I'll be speaking about female suits, since the men got something stylish and form-fitting and useful. Probably had pockets too, the lucky bastards. Originally, for the women, they were these delightful two-piece outfits; a "dress" with full sleeves, but only about knee-length, and a set of ankle-length bloomers. The dress had weights handily sewn into the hem to keep the whole thing from billowing up and possibly exposing a bloomer-clad knee.

Which, in a time when men were aroused by table legs, would've necessitated a lie-down and an ice-pack.

<serious nod>

Anyhow, you know what happens when woolen flannel gets wet? It gets heavy. You know what else gets heavy? *Weights sewn into the hem of your bathing suit.* Women *drowned* to protect their modesty. But this is only good and moral, since nude bathing was outlawed in England in the 1860s.

Nobody tell Raina and Cash, mmmkay?

Now, if you've made it this far in this so-called "Note on Historical Accuracy," then bravo! It should be clear by now that I'm…well, I'm writing RomComs, right? There's history in there, but I'm doing my best to make it *funny*.

Hell, the hero of this book, the "marriage prize" all the

heroines were supposed to want to throw themselves at for the last six books, was named the Duke of *Cashingham*. It's no coincidence I named him the closest I could get to "Cash in Hand" without being *too* obvious.

Although I suppose "DisGrace, the Duke of Cashin-hand" would've worked just as well.

Well, perhaps I'm not so much, "Doing my best to make history funny," as straight-up just *making fun* of history.

Yeah, that's probably right.

Now, I've had my fill of jibes and italics and quotation marks, so it's time to get onto the good stuff.

Thank you, thank you, dear reader, for enjoying all six books in the *Second Chance Manor* series. Scarlett Scott, Merry Farmer and I had the best time writing this series together. We're close friends in real life, and as I'm sure you know, any fun project is even more fun when you're doing it with friends.

(Note to author: Caroline, resist the urge to make a dirty joke here.)

The point is, thank you to everyone who have made these books *the* bestsellers of the summer, and even more appreciation to those who've reviewed already. We are grateful for your support.

For those of you who are *still reading* this, I'm flattered. You must really like me, or at least my writing style. You know what you might like? Figuring out exactly what's going on with Cash's little sister—you know, the hoyden living in London with his mother!

Is it possible Lady Carlotta Merritt, the sister to the Duke of Cashingham, might find happiness with someone who can tame her wild ways? Or perhaps this mysterious hero—whom you've already met, if you've been reading my books—is just the one to encourage her uninhibited nature. Find out in *The Duke's Virgin Sister*, the first in a series about the illegitimate sons of Highland lairds!

And if you're loving my irreverent, laugh-out-loud writing style, I know exactly where to send you next: to read about the rest of the Oliphant Clan! That's right— Raina and Phineas Prince are children of Laird Oliphant, and there's gads of history there!

If you're into super-hot, over-the-top-hilarious RomComs, you'll love **The Hots for Scots** and **Bad in Plaid**. These medieval romps (OMG so many naughty jokes) feature the medieval ancestors of the Oliphant clan, complete with a secret-passage-ridden castle, ghosts foretelling doom, a laird intent on some grandbabies, and more silly puns, anachronistic jokes, and naughty scenes than you can shake a stick at (if you're the kind to shake sticks at stuff).

After you've zoomed through the Oliphants, you're going to want to check out my **Highlander Ever After** series. These are Victorian RomComs, featuring Phineas and Raina's brothers, and all based on fairy tales. You can start with *The Lass Who Lost a Shoe* and go from there.

And now, dear reader, I'll let you go with one more "Thank you!" Please know Scarlett and Merry and I *so* appreciate your love and support, and we would love to hear from you on social media. Do you know we're all admins for the Facebook group, *Historical Harlots*? It's an incredibly active group for readers of naughty historical romance, full of fun posts about history and great book reviews. Come hang out with us!

But first, leave a review for *The Doxy and the Duke!* Second, go pick up one of our other series. *Then* come hang out with us!

See you soon!

OTHER BOOKS BY CAROLINE LEE

Want the scoop on new books? Join Caroline's Cohort, an exclusive reader group! Or sign up for my mailing list by texting "Caroline" to 42828 to get started!

Steamy Scottish Historicals:
   Those Kilted Bastards (3 books)
   Bad in Plaid (6 books)
   The Hots for Scots (8 books)
   Highlander Ever After (3 books)
   The Sinclair Jewels (4 books)
   The Highland Angels (5 books)

Sensual Historical Westerns:
   Black Aces (3 books)
   Sunset Valley (3 books)
   Everland Ever After (10 books)
   The Sweet Cheyenne Quartet (6 books)

Sweet Contemporary Westerns
   Quinn Valley Ranch (5 books)
   River's End Ranch (14 books)
   The Cowboys of Cauldron Valley (7 books)
   The Calendar Girls' Ranch (6 books)

Click **here** to find a complete list of Caroline's books.

*Sign up for Caroline's Newsletter to receive exclusive content and freebies, as well as first dibs on her books! Or if newsletters aren't your thing, follow her on **Bookbub** for a quick, concise new release alert every time she publishes a book!*

ABOUT THE AUTHOR

Caroline Lee has been reading romance for so long that her fourth-grade teacher used to make her cover her books with paper jackets. But it wasn't until she (mostly) grew up that she realized she could *write* it too. So she did.

Caroline is living her own little Happily Ever After in NC with her husband, sons, and new daughter, Princess Wiggles. And while she doesn't so much "suffer" from Pittakionophobia as think that all you people who enjoy touching Band-Aids and stickers are the real weirdos, she *does* adore rodents, and never met a wine she didn't like. Caroline was named Time Magazine's Person of the Year in 2006 (along with everyone else) and is really quite funny in person. Promise.

You can find her at www.CarolineLeeRomance.com.

Made in the USA
Las Vegas, NV
03 September 2021